THE OLD HAS GONE
THE NEW HAS COME!
NEW LIFE

ANDREW WOO YOUNG CHOI

Copyright © 2020 by Andrew Woo Young Choi

All rights reserved. This book or any portion thereof may not be reproduced or transmitted in any form or manner, electronic or mechanical, including photocopying, recording, or by any information storage or retrieval system, without the express written permission of the copyright owner except for the use of brief quotations in a book review or other noncommercial uses permitted by copyright law.

Printed in the United States of America

Library of Congress Control Number: 2020913373
ISBN: Softcover   978-1-64908-076-9
        Hardback   978-1-64908-077-6
        eBook   978-1-64908-075-2

Republished by: PageTurner Press and Media LLC
Publication Date: 07/28/2020

To order copies of this book, contact:

PageTurner Press and Media
Phone: 1-888-447-9651
order@pageturner.us
www.pageturner.us

DEDICATION

Dedicate this book to all who want to live a new life; transformed, friendly, lovely, and hopeful life.

Special thanks to my wife, Sarah, who is my life long soul mate, prayer partner, who always encouraged me to live best life and wholeheartedly support in my time of adversity.

Special thanks to my daughter Josephine and my son David, who are always cheerful, my crown and joy.

Thanks to all supporters in my 30 years of ministry life!

INTRODUCTION

II Corinthians 5:17 says, "Therefore, if anyone is in Christ, he is a new creation; the old has gone, the new has come".

Christian life is renewed and changed life. New means change. So, having a Christian life means new start with a change. With a new life, we could have a hope. We do not have to move to some distant land to begin new life. We just need to be changed inwardly. As the Bible proclaimed, we are new creatures in Christ Jesus. Jon Val jean, in the story of Les Miserables, was a convict and a murderer. The cold and condemning world made his heart increasingly hardened because people hurt him with their prejudice and unforgiving spirit. He endured a wild and difficult 19 years of prison life. Even after having been released, a more severe coldness awaited him in the world. Jon Val jean could have easily become angrier and meaner. However, one priest's forgiveness and unconditional love changed him into an honorable man. Jon Val jean became a marvelous Christian. It was the priest who helped him to start a new life. To this angry and hateful convict who ran away after stealing the priest's silver spoon, the saintly priest gave Jon Val jean even more valuable things and said in front of the police who caught Jon Val jean, "Jon Val jean, I gave you much more than this silver spoon. Here, take all this silver candles." After the police left, the priest said to Jon, "With this silver candles, I will ransom your soul from anger and hatred. I buy your soul from the devil and give your soul back to God." These words and the compassionate heart of the priest changed Jon Val Jean's whole life. That was what

Christ did for us; He ransomed us by His death in order for us to become a changed people.

As I read through the Bible more and more, I am convinced that the whole Bible can be summarized in one sentence of II Corinthians 5: 17, "Therefore, if anyone is in Christ, he is a new creation; the old has gone, the new has come."

When I was a seeker, I wanted to find the way out from emptiness, sense of guilty, and loneliness. I felt like I was locked in a small dark cell of caterpillar. One day, I was hospitalized because I had a severe burn on my head and shoulder. I was unconscious for about two weeks and had a severe pain. I felt like needles were penetrating into my skin of skull. While I was in pain, I realized that Christ died for me. I saw in my dream that Christ went through the pain on the cross for me. I could have related the deep pain of Christ since I felt the sharp pain in my body. More importantly, I realized that His pain is to forgive my sin, all sins of human: to save and to give new life. I believe that realization came to me by the work of the Holy Spirit.

After that experience, my soul was like butterfly that just came out from caterpillar, which transformed into the new creation.

WE ARE NEW CREATION IN CHRIST JESUS
THE OLD HAS GONE! THE NEW HAS COME!

Throughout this book, we can see the contrasts and differences of two lives; old life and the new life.

Life bound in time and space/Life of eternity

Spiritual slavery/Free life

Hopeless life/Hopeful life

Life of anxiety/Peaceful and worry-free life

Worn out life/Energetic life

Coward life/Courageous life,

Depressed life/Joyful life

Live in the past/Life focusing in the future

Earthly life/ Heavenly life in the Kingdom of God

Demander's life/ Servants life

Life end with death/Life eternal

Grudge life/Forgiving and generous life

Complainer' life/Thankful life

Rude life/Humble life

Disobedient life/ obedient life

Life without protection/Protected life

Regretful and resentful life/ Positive and delightful life

Friendless life/ Friendly life

Life of flesh and blood/ Mighty spiritual life

Life of enmity and hatred/Reconciled life

Spiritually widowed life/Redeemed life

Life of cheater/ Life of prince

CONTENTS

Chapter 1: Eternity -Life bound in time and space/Life of eternity 1
    ADAM THROUGH NOAH: The Human limitation and the everlasting life
    Genesis 5:1-32 2

Chapter 2: Life of Freedom 23
    God will give us freedom
    Galatians 5:1-2 24
    God will give us a worry-free life: No Cheap Worries, No Cheap Stress
    Matthew 6: 19-34 31

Chapter 3: New life means to have a life born anew in Spirit. 35
    Jacob changed as a new person, Israel
    Genesis 32:22-32 37
    Jesus personally met with Nicodemus and gives the secret of how to be changed as a new person and born again
    John 3: 1-18 45

Truthful Love
John 3:16 49
True Forgiveness and Fatherly love to the prodigal son
Luke 15, Matthew 18:11–13 53
Jesus met Samaritan women personally and changed her life as a new person
John chapter 4 60

Chapter 4: Perspective that leads to new life 64

Christ Understand and Sympathize
Hebrew 4:14-16 65
The Spit breaks the barrier: By the Spirit of God
Acts Chapter 2 70
The Door is Open Wide: By entering the wide open door
John 3:16-17 74
The City of Refuge: Entering the refuge that God prepared
Numbers Chapter 35 77
God's compassion
Isaiah 49:14-21 80
God's sacrificial love
John 3:16 83
God's holy words transform your life
Acts 12: 1-24 85
GOD SHOWS HIS LOVE IN THREE WAYS:
1st John 4:7-12 89
REDEEMED LIFE OF RUTH
Ruth 4: 1-18 94

Chapter 5: Practice of New life 99

Live a life of the blessing of those who are poor in spirit:
The Blessedness of those who are poor in spirit
Matthew 5: 1-3 101

Live a life of Thanksgiving: Learn to Appreciate
Luke 17: 11-19 106

FORGIVE AS THE FATHER FORGIVES YOU
Luke 15:11-32, Matthew 18:21-35 113

Imitating Christ's Humility
Philippians 2:1-11 118

Love your neighbor: Who is your neighbor?
Luke 10: 25-37 123

Obey your parents
Ephesians 6: 1-4 128

Focus on the future goal
Philippians 3:12-21 132

COMMIT THY WAY TO THE LORD
Psalm 37: 1-7 136

Lord, Give Your Servant a Discerning Heart
1st Kings 3:1-15 141

Live by the Spirit
Zechariah 4: 1-14 145

Look up to God, Who Disciplines and Refines You Like Gold in Times of Suffering
1 Peter 5:5–7, Hebrews 12:5–13, Job 23:10 149

Live a life of victor when life seems unfair
1 Samuel 24: 1-22 155

Live a life of victor when Life seems too tough
Job 1:1–22, John 9:1–12 160

Privileges of New life 169

We will experience miracles in our life: God's Almighty Power Makes Miracles Still Possible
Isaiah 38:1–8 170

We will have a privilege to call God as ABBA FATHER: Our Father in Heaven
Matthew 6: 5-15, Romans 8:15-17 177

We will have real joy and happiness
Psalm 51:1-12 184

We will live bold and courageous life
Acts 1:1-11 189

We will inherit God's Kingdom
John chapter 3, Revelation chapter 21, 22 193

CHAPTER 1

ETERNITY
LIFE BOUND IN TIME AND SPACE/
LIFE OF ETERNITY

BOOK 5: NEW LIFE

ADAM THROUGH NOAH:
The Human limitation and the everlasting life
Genesis 5:1-32

Through Christ's sacrifice on the cross and His resurrection, God restored the fullness of grace and clothed us with His garments of eternal life and eternal blessing. Therefore, let us trust our Lord Jesus Christ who would restore us to perfect happiness and everlasting life.

To Adam, the Lord said, "Because you listened to your wife and ate from the tree about which I commanded you, 'You must not eat of it', 'Cursed is the ground because of you; through painful toil you will eat of it all the days of your life. It will produce thorns and thistles for you and you will eat the plants of the field. By the sweat of your brow you will eat your food until you return to the ground, since from it you were taken; for dust you are and to dust you will return." In this century, environmental problems are very serious because of the development of high technology and complex industries. As a matter of fact, the problems of the environment started from the time of fall have continued until present time. This tendency will continue into the future. Because of the fall of humans, the ground was cursed. So, Paul later said, "Even nature (the whole creation) has been groaning as if in the pains of childbirth right up to the present time. Nature was subjected to frustration, not by its own choice, but by the will of the one who subjected it." (Romans 8:19-23)

In the Garden of delight, work was enjoyable and a delightful. There were no worries, no struggle, no thorns and nothing at all would have prevented human beings from thriving! But now, everything in life seems to go against humans. No more grace, but painful toils and sweat! Eventually we all die! 'To dust' means that humans return to the same material from which God derived the original body of Adam.

Misery in some form exists for all, and misery affects every human being after the fall. As Paul said, "Therefore, just as sin entered the world through one man, and death through sin, and in this way death came to all men." (Romans 5:12) Paul goes on, "As the result of one trespass was condemnation for all humans." (Roman 5:18) Now, we accept death as an inescapable condition of life because it is the destiny of every human being. But, it was not our destiny in the beginning of time. God placed the Tree of Life in the middle of the Garden of Eden so that we all could have the privilege of eternal life. If the first human being did not fall, every person born on this earth would not have to undergo the pain of death. We would always enjoy eternal life. When the Lord drove the humans out of the Garden of Eden, the Lord said, "The man has become like one of us, knowing good and evil. He must not be allowed to reach out his hand and take also from the Tree of life and eat, and live forever." (Genesis 3:22) In this passage, it is clear that the Tree of Life is the tree that would give us everlasting life. But we lost that tree. After God drove out human beings from the Garden of Eden, the Lord guarded the way to the Tree of Life with a flaming sword flashing back and forth. The route to reach the Tree of Life was cut off from us.

Even in the midst of all these miseries, God still showed His mercy. God gave us hope beyond all of those conflicts, pain, and torments. He is still a beaming light that is always shining through the long dark tunnel of life. What is the hope that God showed us after the fall?

First, God helped Adam to restore his relationship with his wife and Eve became the mother of all lives. When the Lord asked Adam why he ate the fruit that God forbid, Adam immediately blamed his wife and said, "I ate it because the woman you allowed me to have as wife gave the fruit. In other words, "I ate the fruit, not because of my own personal fault, but because you did not give me a good wife!" When unpleasant things occur in a family, it is easy for the husband and wife to lay the blame on one another. We often ponder, "Why, Lord, why you give that woman to me" or "Lord, why did you give me that man as my husband?"

But in the aftermath of his being exorcised from the Garden, Adam took personal responsibility and forgave his wife. He named his wife, "Eve", which means the mother of all living of human being. Giving the woman a name signifies that Adam accepted and forgave her. From this point onward, Eve became the mother of all the living. Eve became the mother of every race. We, therefore, have one ancestor. After Noah' day, different races started to emerge. Basically, the races followed the lineages of the three sons of Noah, who were Shem (famous), Ham (passion) and Japheth (beautiful). It was after the incident regarding the fall of the Tower of Babel that many different cultures and languages started to develop. Genesis 9:18 and 10:32 record that, "The sons of Noah who came out of the ark were Shem, Ham and Japheth. These were the sons of Noah, and from them came the people who were scattered over the earth. These are the clans of Noah's sons, according to their lines of descent, within their nations. From these nations spread out over the earth after the flood." So, we all became look different. But if we all trace back to the lines of our genealogy, further than our great-great-grand fathers and mothers, we are all related, because Eve became the mother of all living beings. That is what Biblical genealogy teaches us today. There are two places that mentioned genealogy in the New Testament: in the first chapter of Matthew and in the third chapter of Luke. Luke traced backward and finally recorded, "the son of Seth, the son of Adam."

All human beings have one ancestor, which are Adam and Eve. Look around and if you found someone who looks whole different than you in colors of skins, race, and tradition. Will you believe that they and you have same grandmother, same grandfather? If human beings knew this fact, there would be fewer wars and conflicts between nations. We all remember the cruelty of racism in history and what happened between races. There are so much more cruelty in these 21st century because of racism. If only we all realize that we have same ancestor (Adam and Eve), and so we were therefore interrelated, we would all be able to be more acceptable of one another. I believe that the ability to assimilate the diversity of all cultures and races would be the strength of future USA and this global community and this acceptance would start with the acknowledgment that we all have one ancestor, which are Adam and Eve and by remembering that, somewhere, we all are related, even though our roots span centuries.

Second, God already planned the best remedy for the restoration from the feeling of guilt and shame. Adam and Eve found themselves naked. They were so ashamed that they tried to hide their shame with the leaves of fig trees. The gesture was to cover their sin and guilt. However, as the sun rose, the leaves withered. So Adam and Eve had to hide among the trees. This story symbolically tells us that we cannot cover our sins with our own efforts. There is no resolution for sin when we try to solve with our wisdom and ability. The Lord God made garments of skin clothes for Adam and his wife. The skin clothes were much better suited than the leaves of a fig tree. The clothes made by skins are warm, sturdy and they look good! Most of all, it was necessary to shed the blood of the animals to get these skin clothes, and with these sacrifice God was able to cover Adam and Eve's shame and guilt. Therefore, the fact that God covered them with the skins means that only God can take away sin and guilt and this action foreshadowed that God would redeem human beings by the blood of Jesus Christ. People carry enormous sense of guilt in their deep mind. If we realize that Christ would cover out sin with His thick skin, and forgiveness, we would not experience those pain caused by guilt consciences. I want you to realize that the blood of Jesus Christ would cover all our sins, shame, and guilt.

Thirdly, God showed that there is a possibility to have a long life, and furthermore, to live forever. In the genealogy from Adam to Noah, I believe that you have already found something strange. Wow, they lived a long time! Who lived the longest and for how many years? It was Methuselah who lived 969 years (verse 26-27.) Most of them who lived around Adam's days lived longer than 900 years: Adam: 930, Seth: 912, Enosh: 905, Kenan: 910, Mahalalel: 895, Jared: 962,

Lamech: 777, Noah: 950. Noah got three sons at the age of 500. The flood came when Noah was age 600 and he lived 300 more years after the flood.

The span of a human life is about 80 years in contemporary times because of the development of medicine. If someone lives 100 years in our present society, we would consider that a very long life. Some believed that the span of human life shortened after the flood of Noah for the Lord had said, "His days will be 120 years". Other believed that human life was shortened after Noah's days, because God allowed humans to eat meat after that period in history. Vegetarians would like this theory. Anyway, after this period of long life, the life span was shortened: Sarah: 127, Abraham: 175, Moses: 120

How would you like it, if you could live more than 900 years?

To live a long and healthy life regarded as a blessing from God in the Holy Bible just like in other cultures. (Proverbs 3: 1-2, 4:10, Psalm 91:16, Proverbs 16:31, Ephesians 6:2-3, Deuteronomy 30:20) "Listen my son, accept what I say, and the years of your life will be many." (Proverbs 4:10) George Muller, who was the father of many orphans, lived 90 years and he enjoyed the long healthy life. He said that the secrets of having a long life were these: 1) live a pure and simple life 2) do not commit any sins where you would feel ashamed of yourself 3) have a positive self-image and have a positive relationship with God 5) love the word of God 6) live joyfully, especially enjoy the work of God.

The significant thing about those that people lived very long was that these people knew the Lord. (Genesis 4:26) Men began to call upon the name of the Lord during the period when the human lived ling life. In this period, humankind had lived in an environment that had not been polluted by sin. These people lived in a relatively graceful period. Although they lived long life, they also had to experience the sting of death. In these genealogies of Adam through Noah, the statement of 'then, he died' continued and this phrase repeated eight times: "He lived long, then, he died." In addition, their life was like our life; there were toils in the ground that the Lord had cursed. No matter how much you are blessed in this earthly life, you will experience the emptiness of those when glory passes away. That is why God gives us the yearning for the eternity. Compare the life in this earth, the eternity is incomparably long and we have to think very seriously, 'Where do I spend those eternal days'.

However, there was one person who had never experienced the death. His name was Enoch. He walked with God three hundred years. And then, he did not exist any longer in the world, because God took him away. The book of Hebrews in the New Testament described Enoch's life like this: "By faith Enoch was taken from this life, so that he did not experience death; he could not be found, because God had taken him away. Before he was taken, he was commended as one who pleased God. " (Hebrews 11:5) Enoch lived 365 years on this earth and enjoyed to walk with God – then was taken away to heaven. His life is the prelude of the everlasting life of the believers of Christ who had a victory at the battle with the death.

God has set a yearning for eternity in the hearts of men" (Ecclesiastes 3:1-11)

Solomon had every privilege of life. God had blessed Solomon with wisdom and wealth. God gave him power and fame. Solomon complained, however, and became aggravated and even hated life. His heart began to despair. He said, "So I hated life," I thought this could not be in the Holy Bible. However, Solomon's words do not remain in his negative, pessimistic expression. In the next chapter, Solomon and said, "Life is beautiful. There is a time for everything in life: a time for sorrow, a time for happiness, a time for failure and a time for success, because God has made everything beautiful in its time. And God has set a yearning for eternity in the hearts of men" (Ecclesiastes 3:1-11, author paraphrased))

Solomon became pessimistic when he recognized that humankind was limited by a time frame. No matter what they had achieved and what possessions they had, all humans had to die, as it said in scripture, "There is a time to be born and a time to die." We are limited by a time frame. One of the psalms that Moses wrote says, "Life is like an arrow in the archer's bow, it goes fast. Some people live to be eighty, some live longer, but there are lots of toils and agony." (Psalms 90:10)

It is good to recognize the limitations of humankind by a time frame because that realization leads people to yearn for something long-lasting, meaningful, and eternal.

Solomon later said, "Be happy, young man, while you are young, and let your heart give you joy in the days of your youth. But, remember your Creator in the days of your youth, before the days of trouble come" (Ecclesiastes 11:9–12:1).

Although we are bound by time and space, Jesus will give us eternal life. John 7:37 said, "On the last day and the greatest day of the feast, Jesus stood among the crowds and said in a loud voice, 'If a man is thirsty, let him come to Me and drink. Whoever believes in Me, as Scripture has said, 'streams of water will flow from within him or her.'"

Isaiah 55:1 says, "Come, all who are thirsty, come to the waters, and you who have no money, come and buy and eat. Buy wine and milk without money and without cost. Why spend money on what is not bread and your labor on what does not satisfy? Listen, to Me and eat what is good and your soul will delight in the richest of fare."

Christ gives hope of the everlasting life.

The story of the Samaritan woman and Jesus is one of the most famous stories in the Bible. It begins in John 4. Jesus was walking on a long journey through Samaria, the hot desert. He was thirsty and hungry. Soon he arrived in a town in Samaria called Sychar, where there was Jacob's well. (Joseph inherited this well) Jesus was so tired that he just sat down by the well. It was about the sixth hour—around noon in our measurement of time. Jesus was so thirsty. He asked the Samaritan woman, "Will you give me a drink?" The Samaritan woman said to Jesus very unkindly, "You are a Jew, and I am a Samaritan woman. How can you ask me for a drink?" She was very unkind because Jews never associated with Samaritans. Jesus answered her, "If you knew the gift of God and who it is that asks you for a drink, you would have asked him, and he would have given you living water."

Jesus is the Creator. His nationality was Jewish. His gender was man. This woman was Samaritan, a human, and a woman. There are many differences here. However, Jesus and the Samaritan woman had one common need—something to quench their thirst. Jesus needed water to quench his physical thirst; the woman needed it spiritually. In response to Jesus's asking for water, this woman, who always came to the well of Jacob, now asked Jesus one question: "Are you greater than our father, Jacob?"

Why would a Samaritan woman, who came often to Jacob's well, ask Jesus this very meaningful question: "Are you greater than our father, Jacob?" Why do you think this woman kept coming to Jacob's well? Why did she ask this question? She asked because she needed the water that would sustain her life, a sense of belongingness, and the love that lasts forever.

This story tells us that humans have three basic needs: physical, emotional, and social—a sense of belonging to a group to depend on each other; someone from whom they can receive love and give love. We cannot deny these three needs, but we have to recognize that even though we possesses physical, emotional, social needs, without Christ we would be still thirsty. Jesus said, "Everyone who drinks this water will be thirsty again."

Isaiah said, "Why spend money on what is not bread and expend your labor on what does not satisfy?" (Isaiah 55:2). Success in one's career, personal achievement, economical stability, recognition, friendship, and a happy marriage—we value all of these physical and emotional desires, and it is important to have those desires. However, as we have experienced, we get an empty feeling even after we obtain those things that we really wanted. We climb the mountain to reach our goals and successes. We thought that we would be perfectly happy once we had achieved those goals. But that satisfaction does not last long. We should go further, succeed more, and achieve more to quench our thirst for personal gain. It is like drinking salty water—the more you drink, the less your thirst is quenched.

I've sometimes wondered, "Why can't humans be perfectly satisfied?" The answer is, that is how we are created. God made us to depend on him for our spirituality, our eternity. As the book of Ecclesiastes said, "God has set eternity in the hearts of humankind." When we're born, God that put the desire, the yearning for eternity in our conscious and subconscious. Only God, who is eternal, can quench our thirst for eternity. Jesus said, "Whoever drinks this water will be thirsty again, but whoever drinks the water I give him will never thirst. Indeed, the water I give him will become a spring of water welling up to eternal life" (John 4:13–14).

What does this mean? Why does the water that Jesus gives become a spring of water welling up to eternal life?

It means that Christ's love is perfect, spiritual, eternal. So Christ's love is spiritual drink for us. Humans need sincere and everlasting love. When the Samaritan woman heard about the spring of water welling up to eternal life, she said to Christ, "Sir, give me this water, so that I won't get thirsty again." Jesus told her, "Go, call your husband and come back." She replied, "I have no husband." Jesus said to her, "You are right when you say you have no husband. The fact is, you have had five husbands, and the man you now have is not your husband. What you have said is quite true" Either the woman was unfaithful or the husbands were unfaithful. Whatever the case, this woman had lots of experience with broken marriages. As a result, she had experienced much hurt. Whenever she drew water from Jacob's well, she thought about the story of Jacob, who was a sincere and faithful man. Jacob loved only one woman.

Jacob worked for fourteen years for one woman, Rachel. Day and night, he fed the flocks of Rachel's father. He was given no salary, no reward for his effort. He toiled just because he loved Rachel. Jacob looked foolish to others, but to the Samaritan woman who had broken off from five husbands, Jacob was admirable because Jacob's love was sincere and faithful. This is another facet of the Samaritan woman's question to Christ, "Are you greater than Jacob?" With this question, she was actually asking, "Is your love, God's love, more sincere and more faithful than Jacob's love for Rachel?" As Christ's love quenches the spirit of this woman, His love, agape love, will quench our thirst for the eternity.

The second meaning of Jesus saying, "I will give you springs of water welling up to eternal" is that Christ will give us a perfect sense of belonging. To the Samaritan woman, Jacob's well was not just a place to draw water; it also was more than a physical well. This woman was looking for a sense of belongingness at Jacob's well. Think about why she was asking the unusual question, "Are you greater than our father, Jacob?" She emphasized the fact that Jacob was her ancestor, and she was one of the children of Jacob. And she noted that Jacob himself drank from the same well, as did his sons and his flocks and herds as well. She also stated that Jacob handed over the well to her people, the Samaritans.

I would like to tell you the history of the relationship between the Jews and the Samaritans. The Jews and the Samaritans were the same race, the same nation. In 722 BC, they were divided into two sections. The Jews inhabited the southern part of Israel; the Samaritans inhabited the northern territory. The Jewish people were very exclusive and lived in a closed society. They despised the Samaritans, even though they lived in the same country. The Jews ostracized the Samaritans and treated them as third-class citizens because the Samaritans intermarried with foreign nations, especially with Assyrians.

Following the invasion by Assyria into the northern kingdom of Israel in 722 BC, the Israelites in northern Israel, which we call

Samaritans, intermarried with the Assyrians. The Jews were intolerant of the mixture of the Samaritan and Assyrian cultures. The hostility lasted for a very long time. Even after six centuries, in 120 BC, when the Samaritans built a temple in their city, Gerzim, the southern Jews attacked the Samaritans and destroyed the entire temple. The southern Jews treated the Samaritans as their worst enemy.

But the Samaritan was not foreigners; they were Jews. They could not be Romans; they could neither be Greeks nor any other nation because they were Jews. But at the same time, they were rejected by their own people and would not be accepted as Jewish. They were on the fringe of two different nations. And the sad fact was that Samaritans could not have any sense of belonging. That was their dilemma. That was why this woman kept on saying, "You are a Jew. I am a Samaritan woman. Our fathers, yours and mine, were Jews. You may deny it, but we belong to each other." Whenever she came to Jacob's well, she reminded herself, "I belong to Jacob." And she said to herself, "No matter what the Jewish people say, we are all the descendants of Jacob. Abraham is my ancestor."

Have you experienced rejection from others of the same race? Have you been excluded from their association and their fellowship, even if you live within their neighborhood? Have you been ignored because of your differences to them? Or have you excluded others who want to associate with you? Exclusion causes a terrible, pitiful feeling. That was just what the Samaritan woman felt. She felt ostracized, excluded, and alone. Do you feel ostracized or excluded, even from Christians?

The need to belonging, to be a part of something, tells us that we humans are social beings. In the famous story Robinson Crusoe, Robinson Crusoe did not like people because there were many conflicts in human relationships. To resolve this problem, he went to an isolated, distant island and lived alone. However, Crusoe learned that humans are social beings and need people around, even though there were ongoing conflicts in human relationship. With this newfound insight, Robinson Crusoe came back to society. Humans need people, a group in which they can belong. Human tend to be selective. We like certain people, but we do not like others. We prefer this, and we do not prefer that. However, Jesus, in his actions, in his words, and in his heart, embraces everybody. He accepts the ones who are rejected by others. God accepts us as we are and regards us as his children. In Christ Jesus, we drink of his acceptance of all people, and it will be a spring of water welling up to eternal life.

The third meaning of Jesus saying, "I will give you springs of water welling up to eternal" is that we will have eternal life in Christ, literally. The first reason that the Samaritan woman kept on coming to the Jacob's well was because she needed the water. It was a symbolic way of telling us that people need basic physical things. We wake up early in the morning and go to work. We work hard for our family to bring bread to the family's table. We are similar to the Samaritan woman, who kept on going to Jacob's well to draw water. We are consistently needful beings. We consume things; at the same time, we are consumable beings who will end our lives as ashes.

Christ, however, will give eternal life to us. We will not be bound by time when we join with his eternity. When we pass from this life, we will continue on that right path forever in eternity. We will not be bound by time. We will live a spiritual life, now and forever.

Jesus is the true bread of life. His words and actions are the water we can drink that will lead us to eternity. If we seek only material things, we will die. There is nothing material or emotional in this world that can perfectly satisfy us or launch us into our eternity. In God, however, we will always have eternity. Jesus gives to us water, which becomes the spring of water that wells up and transports us to everlasting life. The everlasting life, the springing of water that lasts forever, is the privilege that we possess since we became newborn creatures in Christ. I pray that God will give a spring of water that wells up to you. In Jesus's name, I pray. Amen.

Christ will give you eternal life I: Spring of water
John chapter 3

Now, I would like to tell you the story of the Samaritan woman and Jesus. It is one of the most famous stories in the Bible. I believe that you have often heard this story. It begins in John's gospel chapter four. Now, Jesus was walking and had long journey going through Samaria, the hot desert. He was thirsty and hungry. Soon He arrived to a town in Samaria called Sychar, where there was Jacob's well. (Joseph inherited this well) Jesus was so tired that he just sat down by the well. And it was about the sixth hour; it is around noontime in our measurement of time. Jesus was so thirsty. He asked the Samaritan woman, "Will you give me a drink?" The Samaritan woman said to Jesus very unkindly, "You are a Jew and I am a Samaritan woman. How can you ask me for a drink?" She was very unkind because Jews never associated with Samaritans. Jesus answered her, "If you knew the gift of God and who it is that asks you for a drink, you would have asked Him and He would have given you living water." Jesus is the Creator, His nationality was Jewish, His gender was man. This woman was Samaritan, a human and a woman. There are many differences here. However, Jesus and the Samaritan woman had one common need. Both needed something to quench their thirst – Jesus needs water to quench his thirsty - this woman, spiritually. As a response for Jesus' asking for water, this woman who always came to the well of Jacob, now asked Jesus one question, "Are you greater than our father, Jacob?"

Let us take a moment to think of why a Samaritan woman, who kept on coming to Jacob's well, asked Jesus a very meaningful question: "Are you greater than our father, Jacob?" Why do you think this woman kept on coming to Jacob's well? Why had she asked Jesus, "Are you greater than Jacob?" She asked this question because she needed the water that would sustain her life, sense of belongingness, and the love that lasts forever. In summary, this story tells us symbolically that humans have three basic needs, economic, social sense of belongingness to a group to depend on each other, and love, someone whom they can receive love and give love. We cannot deny these three needs, but we have to recognize the fact that EVEN THOUGH WE POSSESS ALL THOSE THREE ELEMENTS, AND EVEN IF ALL OF THOSE THREE PHYSICAL AND EMOTIONAL NEEDS WERE MET, WE WOULD STILL BE THIRSTY as Jesus said, "Everyone who drinks this water will be thirsty again."

Isaiah said, "Why spend money on what is not bread and expend your labor on what does not satisfy? (Isaiah 55:2) Success in one's career, personal achievement, economical stability, recognition, friendship, and a happy marriage! We value all of those physical and emotional desires and it is important to have those desires. However, as we have experienced, we get an "empty feeling" even after we obtain those things that we really wanted. We climb the mountain to reach our goals and successes. We thought that we would be perfectly happy once we had achieved those goals. But, that satisfaction does not last long. We have to go further, succeed more and achieve more to quench our thirst for personal gain. It is like drinking salty water. The more you drink, the less your thirst is quenched.

I sometimes wondered, "Why can't humans be perfectly satisfied?" The answer is; that is how we are created. God made us to depend on Him for our spirituality, our eternity. As the book of Ecclesiastes said, "God has set eternity in the hearts of humankind." When were born, it was God that put the desire, the yearning for eternity in our conscious and in our subconscious. Only God, who is eternal, can quench our thirst for eternity. Jesus said, "Whoever drinks this water will be thirsty again, but whoever drinks the water I give him will never thirst. Indeed, the water I give him will become a spring of water welling up to eternal life."(John 4:13-14)

What does this mean? Why does the water that Jesus gives become a spring of water welling up to eternal life?

It means first that Christ's love is perfect, spiritual, eternal. So, Christ's love is spiritual drink for us. Human needs sincere and everlasting love. When the Samaritan woman heard about the spring of water welling up to eternal life, she asked Christ, "Sir, give me this water, so that I won't get thirsty again." Jesus told her, "Go, call your husband and come back." She replied, "I have no husband." Jesus said to her, "you are right when you say you have no husband. The fact is, you have had five husbands, and the man you now have is not your husband. What you have said is quite true" Either the woman was unfaithful or the husbands were unfaithful. Whatever the case, this woman had lots of experience with broken marriage. As a result, she had experienced much hurt. Whenever she drew water from Jacob's well, she thought about the story of Jacob who was sincere and faithful man Jacob, who loved only one woman.

As you know, Jacob worked for fourteen years for one woman, Rachel. Day and night, he fed the flocks of Rachel's father. He was given no salary, no reward for his effort. He toiled just because he loved Rachel. Jacob looked foolish to others, but to the Samaritan woman who had broken off from five husbands, Jacob was admirable because Jacob's love was sincere and faithful. This is another facet of the Samaritan woman's question to Christ, "Are you greater than Jacob? With this question, she was actually asking, "Is your love, God's love, more sincere and more faithful than Jacob's love for Rachel?" As Christ' love quenches the spirit of this woman, His love, Agape love will quench our thirst for the eternity.

Second meaning of what Jesus saying, "I will gives you springs of water welling up to eternal" is that Christ will give us perfect sense of belongingness. To the Samaritan woman Jacob's well was not just a place to draw water; it was more than a physical well. This woman was looking for a sense of belongingness at Jacob's well. Think about why she was asking the unusual question, "Are you greater than our father, Jacob? She emphasized the fact that Jacob was her ancestor and she was one of the children of Jacob. And she noted that Jacob, himself, drank from the same well, as did his sons and his flocks and his herds as well. She also stated that Jacob handed over the well to her people, the Samaritans.

I would like to tell you the history of the relationship between the Jews and the Samaritans. Actually, the Jews and the Samaritans were the same race, the same nation. At BC 722, they were divided into two sections. The Jews inhabited the southern part of Israel, the northern territory by the Samaritans. As you know the Jewish people were very exclusive and they live in a closed society. They despised the Samaritans, even though they lived in the same country. The Jews ostracized the Samaritans and treated them as third class citizens because the Samaritans intermarried into foreign nations, especially with Assyrians. Following the invasion by Assyria into the Northern kingdom of Israel in 722 BC, the Israelites in Northern Israel, which we call Samaritans, intermarried with the Assyrians. The Jews were intolerant of the mixture of the Samaritan and Assyrian cultures. The hostility lasted for a very long time. Even after six centuries in 120 BC, when the Samaritans built a temple in their city, Gerzim, the southern Jews attacked the Samaritans and destroyed the entire temple. The Southern Jews treated the Samaritans as their worst enemy.

But, the Samaritan were not foreigners, they were Jews. They could not be Romans; they could neither be Greeks nor any other nation, because they were Jews. But at the same time, they were rejected by their own people and would not be accepted as Jewish. They were on the fringe of two different nations. And the sad fact was that Samaritans could not even have any belongingness. That is their dilemma. That was why, this woman kept on saying that "You are a Jew, I am a Samaritan woman. Our fathers, yours and mine, were Jews. You may deny it, but we belong to each other. Whenever, she came to Jacob's well she reminded herself of the fact that "I belong to Jacob" And she said to herself, "No matter what the Jewish people says, we are all the descendants of Jacob, Abraham is my ancestor."

Have you experienced rejection from others of the same race? Have you been excluded from their association and their fellowship even you live within their neighborhood? Have you been ignored because of your differences in comparison to them? Or have you excluded others who want to associate with you? " Exclusion causes a terrible, pitiful feeling. That was just what the Samaritan woman felt. She felt ostracized, excluded and alone. Do you feel ostracized, excluded even from Christian?

The need to belongingness, to be a part of something, tells us that we humans are social beings. In the famous story, Robinson Crusoe, Robinson Crusoe did not like people because there were many conflicts in human relationships. To resolve this problem, he went go to an isolated, distant island and lived alone. However, Crusoe learned that humans are social beings and need people around even though there were ongoing conflicts in human relationship. With this newfound insight, Robinson Crusoe came back to society. Humans need people, a group in which they can belong. Human tend to be selective. We like certain people but we do not like others. We prefer this and we do not prefer that. However, Jesus in His actions, in His words, and in His heart embraces everybody. He accepts the ones who are rejected by others. God accepts us as we are and regards us as His children. In Christ Jesus, we drink of His acceptance of all people and it will be a springs of water welling up to eternal life.

Thirdly, we will have eternal life in Christ, literally. The first reason that the Samaritan woman kept on coming to the Jacob's well was because the woman needed the water. It was a symbolic way of telling us that people need basic physical things. We wake up early in the morning and go to work. We work hard for our family to bring bread to the family's table. We are similar to the Samaritan woman who kept on going to Jacob's well to draw water. We are consistently needful beings. We are consuming things, at the same time; we are consumable being that would end our life as ashes.

However, Christ will give eternal life to us. We will not be bound by time when we join with His eternity. When we pass from this life, we will continue in that right path forever in eternity. We will not be bound by time. We will be living a spiritual life now and forever.

Jesus is the true bread of life. His words and actions are the water of which we can drink and lead us to eternity. If we seek only material things, we will die. There is nothing, either material or emotional things, in this world that can perfectly satisfy us nor can launch us into our eternity. However, In God, we will always have eternity. Jesus gives to us water, which becomes the spring of water that wells up and transports us to everlasting life. The everlasting life, the springing of water that last forever, is the privilege that we would possess since we become new born in Christ. I pray that God would give spring of water lead to the eternity to you today. In Jesus Name, I pray. Amen.

I've met one very sincere Christian. They were going to have their first baby very soon. It was to be a daughter. However, something happened and the baby could not be removed from the womb and the baby died. The couple experienced tremendous sorrow and grief. They worried about the eternal destiny of the baby asked a question, "Where is our baby going to spend her time in her eternal destiny?" The mother had learned that those who never accepted Christ as their Savior would be destined to remain in a horrible place. Her question was, "Is my baby going to spend her eternity at hell?" I shared my belief and told her, "All human beings fall under the category of Adam's sin. All are born with sin. However, your baby and all children who were not yet exposed to the temptation of sin are innocent. Therefore, God will regard them as angels. So, your daughter will be in heaven with the Lord."

Whatever your beliefs are, we are all limited human beings and we do not know our eternal destiny and once in a while we wonder about it.

Years ago, a Polish priest named Gerogu got the Nobel Prize in literature for the book entitled, "The 25th Hour". The setting was during the period when the Germans persecuted the Jews. The main character had a last name, which was similar to a Jewish name. But, actually the man was not a Jew. Nonetheless, he was thrown into prison and separated from his family. He was faced with many troubles. In his novel, Georogu tried to describe a human being who had lost his ground of existence. He had no place to stand. The title of his novel, The 25th Hour, matched the story very well. All humankind is bounded in time and space. We all live in the two dimensions. If we want to live in the twenty-fifth hour, we would be like a train derailed.

In today's scriptures, Solomon explained about the "time factor" in our lives in various ways. He said, "There is a time for everything, and a season for every activity under heaven: a time to be born and a time to die."

The writer of the book of Ecclesiastes is Solomon and he wrote two wisdom literatures, one is Proverbs and the other is Ecclesiastes. In the first two chapters of Ecclesiastes, he expressed lots of his frustration and agony in a very negative way, "Meaningless! Meaningless! Everything is meaningless. What does man gain from all his labor at which he toils under the sun? All things are wearisome, more than one can articulates. The eye never has enough of seeing, or the ear its fill of hearing. There is noting new under the sun." He asked the question, "Is there anything of which one can say, Look this is something new? No! Solomon continued in aggravation and said, "Wisdom, knowledge even pleasure and hard work for the good life are all meaningless! About wisdom, 'I thought to myself, 'Look, I have grown and increased in wisdom more than anyone who has ruled over Jerusalem before me. Then I applied that wisdom to life and it worked perfectly, but I learned that this too is a chasing after the wind. Will the man who comes after me be a wise man or a fool? Yet he will have control over all the work into which I have poured my effort and skill under the Sun."

He kept on saying concerning pleasure, "I built houses for myself and planted nice vineyards, gardens, parks, and fruit trees. I hired many workers who worked for me. I also owned more herds and flocks than anyone in Jerusalem before me. I gathered silver and gold. I became greater. My heart took delight in all my work, and this was the reward for all my labor. Yet when I surveyed all that my hands had done and what I had toiled to achieve, everything was meaningless, a chasing after the wind, nothing was gained under the sun, because I must leave them to the one who comes after me."

Solomon had every privilege of life. God had blessed Solomon with wisdom and wealth. God gave him power and fame. However, Solomon complained, became aggravated and even hated life. Becoming more aggravated and his heart began to despair. He said, 'So I hated life' I myself thought that this could not be in the Holy Bible. However, Solomon's words do not remain in his negative, pessimistic expression. Solomon progresses to the next chapter and said, "life is beautiful. There is a time for everything in life: a time for sorrow, a time for happiness, a time for failure and a time for success, because God has made everything beautiful in its time. And God has set a yearning for eternity in the hearts of men" (3:10)

Solomon became pessimistic when he recognized that humankind was limited by the time frame. No matter what they had achieved and what possessions they had, all humans had to die as it said in scripture, "There is a time to be born and a time to die." We are limited by a time frame. One of the Psalms that Moses wrote says, "Life is like an arrow in the archer's bow, it goes fast. Some people live to be 80, some live longer, but there are lots of toils and agony."

It is good to recognize the limitation of humankind by a time frame, because that realization would leads people to yearn for something long-lasting, meaningful, and furthermore, eternal. So, now returning to Solomon, Solomon later said, "Be happy, young man, while you are young, and let your heart give you joy in the days of your youth. But, remember your Creator in the days of your youth, before the days of trouble come" (Ecclesiastes 11:9- 12:1)

Although we are bounded by time and space, Jesus will give us eternal life. John 7: 37 said; "On the last day and the greatest day of the feast, Jesus stood among the crowds and said in a loud voice, 'If a man is thirsty, let him come to Me and drink. Whoever believes in Me, as Scripture has said, 'streams of water will flow from within him or her.'

" In Isaiah 55:1, it says, "Come, all who are thirsty, come to the waters, and you who have no money, come and buy and eat. Buy wine and milk without money and without cost. Why spend money on what is not bread and your labor on what does not satisfy? Listen, to Me and eat what is good and your soul will delight in the richest of fare." Our privilege of having a new life in Christ is the life everlasting.

CHAPTER 2
LIFE OF FREEDOM

[1]

---
[1] https://www.bing.com/images/search?view(Accessed on 5/16/2020)

BOOK 5: NEW LIFE

God will give us freedom
Galatians 5:1-2

Freedom is so important to us that people are willing to gives their life to earn the freedom. If we look at the history of Israel, we find that there were not many years that the Israelites had lived in a free country. From ancient times, they were in slavery, whether in Egypt, Babylon, Persia, Greece, and Rome. The Israelites enjoyed the full privilege of living in a free country only during the period when King David and King Solomon reigned. Another short period that they had enjoyed the freedom was during the time of the Maccabees. This struggle of the Israelites for gaining religious freedom and political independence was successful for only a few decades. They fought hard to keep their freedom. However, their last efforts ended when the Roman Army invaded Jerusalem and destroyed the Jerusalem Temple.

One of the heroic stories of Maccabee and his followers was the time when they fought against the Romans at the rock fortress of Massada. The fortress of Massada was a natural and well-situated stronghold of the Maccabees. The Roman Army could not conquer Masada. So, the Romans cut all the supply routes of all food and other essentials, thinking that the Maccabees would surrender. But, a few days later, when the Romans climbed up the Masada fortress, they found that all the people - old, young, men and women, even children had taken their lives. They chose death rather than to live in slavery. They wanted to remain as free people. But there was no way to achieve this in reality. They found an alternative, and it was death in order to be free. It was a sad story. When I read that account, I realized how important it is to have freedom; religious freedom and political independence. Therefore, to the Jews who had a background of a continuous struggle for freedom, the words, 'free or slavery' were very sensitive words. There was one occasion when Jesus and the Jewish leaders had a serious dialogue about freedom. Jesus told them, "You need to have freedom." The Jewish leaders were so upset about that statement and responded to Christ in this way, 'How can you tell us that we need to be free. We are Abraham's descendants. We have never been in slavery.' (John chapter 8) Christ never tried to deny their strong confidence nor did He wish to hurt their pride. Rather, He simply told them how important it was to have spiritual freedom IN HIM. Christ continued, "I tell you the truth, everyone who sins is a slave to sin. Now, a slave has no permanent place in the family, but a son belongs to it forever. So, if the Son sets you free, you will be free indeed."

It is important to have freedom in every area of our life, economic, political, religious, health, so on. But the most important truth to remember is that Christ is the only One who can give us real freedom. I hear many people nowadays striving for economic freedom. I agree that we need to have a certain amount of economic status to have a decent life. I agree that when we have to count every penny to pay the bills, we cannot enjoy freedom. However, as Jesus Christ said, "we cannot be really free until we are free from sin." Even if we have all other freedoms and yet possessed by guilt feelings, hatred or become bound by sinful desires, or regrets about things passed, we are indeed not free.

After the fall of Adam, there are continuing tensions and struggles for humankind because of the enmity and animosity between humankind and the Satan. There are toils and struggles for survival and wars between nations, diseases and natural disasters. When sin entered into the lives of humankind, agony and sorrow came into the lives of all human beings. And then finally, all destined to die. As the book of Hebrews says, "It is appointed for men to die once, and the most horrible thing is that after death, we all have to stand before God for His judgment." Even if we have everything in the world, we will never completely free. However, Christ paid the full penalty of our sins and found the way to free us from spiritual slavery. God gives us the opportunity to have glorious freedom in Christ Jesus. Total freedom was given to us by the grace of God, yet we need to respond to have the freedom that Christ gained for us. Christ said, "If you hold my teaching, you are really my disciples. Then you will know the truth and the truth will set you free. " (John 8:31)

Everything good things come through grace and grace is free. Then, why do we have to live an ethical and responsible life? I would like to answer to that question with the illustration of a train and a rail. If the train is off its rail, the train can no longer have the freedom to run. Christ's teachings are like a rail for us and we are the train in His rail. If we hold onto Christ's teaching and run with His Words, we are as free as the train in the rail. But if we are derailed, there will be destruction and you cannot move even an inch. To have a full freedom, we have to hold the teaching of Christ. When others scorned and condemned the woman caught in adultery, Christ gave full grace to the woman who was in the shameful situation. At the same time, Christ gave her clear direction of new way of life of truth. Christ told her to change her life style and to be free from sin and to live in the way Christ showed and pursue righteousness.

When you do not have any other options in the world to achieve the full freedom of life, and even if you have tried all avenues, if you still have no solution in your efforts, Christ is another alternative that you can try. Instead of concentrating on problems and dwelling on thoughts of the past or guilt or wrong desires, remember the truth of forgiveness and righteousness and hope that Christ would give you an ultimate solution. Holy Scripture guarantees that we will have real, full and total freedom as Jesus promised to us like following, "If the Son sets you free, you will be free indeed."

Paul found that the church members of Galatians misunderstood the Christianity and still bore the burdens of keeping the expired laws and the yoke of slavery. He said, "If it is for freedom that Christ has set us free. Stand firm, then, and do not let yourselves be burdened by the yoke of slavery." With this statement, Paul was emphasizing that the single most important reason for having a new life in Christ is for freedom. Is your Christian life full of joy and freedom or is it another extra burden? If we do not enjoy the full privileges of being in God's grace and restricted by unnecessary rules and regulation and having an extra burden, it is contrary to the original intent of God's calling us into Christ. Christian life will be more burden than live as non-Christian, if we do not enjoy the full freedom being in Christ. That is what Paul said; "It is for freedom that Christ has set us free. Stand firm, then, do not let yourselves be burdened by the yoke of slavery."

With the words in Romans 8:1-2, I want to talk more specifically about freedom that we get in Christ. "Therefore, there is no condemnation for those who are in Christ Jesus, because through Christ Jesus the law of the Spirit of life set me free from the law of sin and death." (Romans 8:1-2)

The most important blessing of being a Christian is the freedom from condemnation of the sin and spiritual death. Apostle Paul made the comparison of 'the law of the Spirit' and 'the law of sin and death' in these verses. The law ('Nomos' in Greek) mentioned here does not mean the Law of Moses or more than 600 regulations that come from the Old Testament. In here, the law can be translated as 'norms' in English and it means 'principle/rule'. There are principles and rules in nature and these rules control life, nature and the cosmos. Let's take the principle of gravity as an example. Water never flows upstream. It always flows downward. If there were no principles of gravity, the water of the ocean would come upon the earth and would sweep over us, it would ruin the whole earth. Can we avoid the law of gravity? As far as we are remaining in the realm of gravity of this earth, we could never avoid it naturally. You can jump high, but no matter how high you jump up, you will ultimately come down.

Likewise, we can never avoid the principle of sin and death with our own ability because the law/principle of sin and death is ever stronger than our will to live righteously. Apostle Paul even in his old age and after having become a mature Christian still struggled with sin. He confessed his frustration, "I have the desire to do what is good, but I cannot carry it out! I, in my inner being, delight in God's law, but I see another law at work in the members of my body, waging war against the law of my mind and making me a prisoner of the law of sin. What a wretched man I am! Who will rescue me from the body of death!" (Romans 7: 18-24)

Like gravity, sin pulls us down. It controls us. Unless we apply any other special rule, we should be under the 'principle of sin and death'. In the final stages of our life, we will be condemned with death. In a one part of Psalm, Moses wrote, "Life flies fast and life lasts only sixty to eighty years, but it is full of suffering and sorrow." Nobody in the world could be free from the law of sin and death.

However, when we are "In Christ", different principle applies in our lives. This is the principle of the Spirit of life. When the law of the Spirit of life is applied and when we are in Christ, we live in a totally different realm. I would like to give you pictures that closely illustrate the meaning of the word "In-Christ." These are very important words, because these words will determine our eternal destiny. Whether we are IN or OUT of Christ makes our life totally different.

'In Christ' means 'Unified with Christ'

What is our situation before being united with Christ? It is isolation; we are set apart and completely lost. We have loneliness. We are destined to die and be condemned. Do you remember the story of Noah's Ark? People of those days lived only by the flesh. They were sinful and violent. So, God grieved. That means God regretted having created humankind. God, who made human beings, was in a quandary. When we watch the news of CNN about the violence, cruelty and heartless crimes happening in this world, we sighed and said, 'How could such evil people exist?' God even repented for having made such evil people. When we hear shocking news presented over and over these days, we just wonder why!

God's heart was filled with pain. Eventually, He decided to wipe out all humankind and said, "I will wipe out mankind by water." However, He planned to save Noah and his family and one pair of each type of animals. He commanded Noah to build a "Noah' Ark". This command was extremely difficult to follow because people had never experienced rain in those days. The temperature was always balmy and excellent conditions prevailed. It was neither too hot nor too cold. A proper temperature of dew covered the earth in the morning and the Sun made the dew warm like a heater and it was always perfect weather. The sky always was clear. Noah did not even have a concept of rain. But he obeyed God's command and built the Ark.

When it started to rain and the floodwaters were beginning to invade the earth, Noah and his sons Shem, Ham, Japheth, together with Noah's wife and the wives of the three sons entered the Ark. Following Noah's family, pairs of all creatures that had the breath of life in them came to Noah and entered the Ark. A very important statement follows that, "Then, the Lord shut him IN. Now, they were IN the Ark.". (Genesis 7: 16) When all others who were not IN Noah's Ark were drowned, those who were IN Noah's Ark were saved. Likewise, those who are IN Christ and United with Christ will be saved.

One of the areas that many people misunderstand about the Christianity is God's Sovereignty (God's Will) verses determinism. A few years ago, the when Moslem pilgrimages to Mecca visited their holy city there were too many crowds in the Mecca at the same time period and so the construction fell down. Because of that, many people died. The response of the pilgrimage was, "It was the will of most high". The News reporter asked, "Can it be avoidable disaster?" I believe that God's will is preventing the possible disaster and make the pilgrimage to have safe travel. Even some Christians have the fashion of thought, "Since God is doing it all, we just need to float on it. Since God has determination for our life, we cannot do anything about our life." It is the way of thinking that, since God is determining all, there is no place for our own will. This is fatalism, not believing the sovereignty of God. If we misunderstand the sovereignty of God, then being a Christian is more burden than just living as regular ordinary people. Then, why do we bother to live a Christian life? God do not want to bind us with fatalism. God's will is that 'since we have freedom in Christ, we can have hope and the possibility to make our life better. When most of people think there is no other way for better life, we still can depend on God's sovereignty and hope for the solution because God gave us the alternative. To us, there are alternative when nothing seems to work, that alternative is giving trust to the sovereignty of God. God saved us for this freedom to look at the solution when other' can't. Let me say again that God's will for us is to give us freedom from sin and the power of death and fatalism. Freedom is one of the most important privileges of having a new life in Christ.

God will give us a worry-free life:
No Cheap Worries, No Cheap Stress
Matthew 6: 19-34

Today, I have a good article for you. I once shared this piece at a Wednesday prayer meeting. Allow me to read this article. It was written by Robert J. Hastings and was the cover story of the 'Southern Baptist Bulletin'.

The title of the piece is "No Cheap Worries, No Cheap Stress"

For several years I've been a regular donor at our local blood bank. Each time I go into the clinic, I receive a warm sense of satisfaction. On my last visit they gave me a new donor card. My old one was completely filled. As I replaced the old card in my wallet, I scanned the dates I had donated, the pulse, blood pressure and blood count on each occasion. The records were consistent, varying little through the years. With one exception! One morning in 1981 when I visited the blood bank, my blood pressure went up unexpectedly. For some reason, which I could not recall, it had been a stressful morning. The increase in my blood pressure was undoubtedly emotion-related. As I fingered the card, I tried to remember what had upset me that morning in 1981. But I couldn't. Time had erased the memory. So, I told myself, 'If it isn't important enough to remember, it probably didn't deserve worrying about at the time.' Which is the truth of Job 34:29, 'When he gives quietness, who then can make trouble?' Much of our trouble' is self-made, and not worth the time we fret about it. Emily Dickinson wrote a beautiful poem on this theme. She compared petty thoughts to cheap pottery that falls on the floor and shatters. She concluded that worse than the loss of the plate or cup is the fact that she gave space on her kitchen shelf for 'plated waters' in the first place.

What shall we do with cheap worries, cheap stress? Don't give them the time of day, let alone a niche in our hearts.

What makes you worry, if you do worry? By the way, what exactly is worry? Here is Webster's Dictionary definition, "To cause anxiety; to torment; to vex; to plague; to tear or mangle with teeth. Worry is also a mental disturbance due to care and anxiety."

Worry as 'tearing or mangling with teeth!' is an interesting definition. It must come from the Greek meaning for the word of worry; 'To tear into pieces and parts.' So, when Jesus said 'Do not worry', He meant that the disciples should not tear their hearts into pieces. He meant that they should not be distracted nor divide their concern into many parts. This does not mean that we do not care about our families or our environment. What Jesus was trying to emphasize is that each of us has only one mind, so we can think of only one thought at a time. If something drags you into dividing your concerns, your spirit will be torn down. Worry causes sleep disturbances, eating disorders as well as nagging ill health. Since worry is simply unnecessary and it just harm, not helping to improve or solve the problem, Jesus simply said, "Do not worry. I tell you, do not be anxious about your life, what you shall eat or what you shall drink, nor about your body, what you shall put on."

Jesus also said, "Which of you by being anxious can add one cubit to his span of life?" One cubit is about the length of your wrist to your elbow, a very small distance. Being anxious does not give you the capability of lengthening your life by even a little bit. Worry does not help, but it does do a lot of harm. In the worst case worry destroys us. So, why worry? This is a very logical conclusion. But in reality it is very difficult to stop worrying. Worry just sits in our mind. Jesus knows that overcoming worry is not only a logical matter, since the whole person-emotion, thinking-all involved in worry. So, Christ has suggested the following ways to handle worry. I believe that we can be released from the worry and have peace in our mind if we follow to Christ's suggestion.

How do we overcome the worry?

First, Trust God who cares about you! The apostle Peter said "Cast all your care upon Him, for He cares for you!" I put this scripture verse on the right corner of my computer. Whenever I look at this verse and

I remind myself that God would always take care of me. What a great relief I experience from my burdens! The opposite word of worry is trust. There comes time when we can't do anything but just trusting God. Christ suggested trusting God who cares about your life; "Look at the birds of the air; they neither sow nor reap nor gather into barns, and yet the heavenly Father feeds them. Are you not of more valuable than they?"(Verse 26) "And why are you anxious about clothing? Consider the lilies of the field, how they grow; they neither toil nor spin; yet I tell you, even Solomon in all his glory was not arrayed like one of these. But, if God so clothes the grass of the field, which today is alive and tomorrow is thrown into the oven, will He not much more clothe you, O ye of little faith ?" (Verse 30)

Secondly, acknowledge God who values you as a person who is more important than any other thing in the world, even more important than the universe. You are the most important person in God's sight! More encouraging fact is that He is our Father! I want to remind you verse 26 again. "Look at the birds of the air; they neither sow nor reap nor gather into barns, and yet the heavenly Father feeds them. Are you not of more valuable than they?" So, we can give all of our burdens to Him. Sometimes we do not know what the future holds for us, but we are sure that our Father will take care of our future and us.

Thirdly, focus on the chores of each day. The future tasks will always be there, they are not going anywhere. Make a basic plan for future tasks and events, but focus primarily on the tasks for today. Jesus wants us to plan and estimate the cost and develop the courses of action and think it through. However, we have to know that God is the one who make it happen. So, Jesus said, "therefore, do not be anxious about tomorrow, for tomorrow will be anxious for itself. Let the day's own trouble be sufficient for the day." The New International Version of the Bible translates this concept this way: "Do not worry about tomorrow, for tomorrow will worry about its own things. Sufficient for the day is its own trouble." This is one of my favorite Scriptures. This means that one should focus on this day. One of the main reasons why people suffer and trouble is not because they lack something or they have something to lose, it is because people project in their mind that they are going to lose something. These negative thoughts pile up for months. That negativity, real or imagined, gnaws at the core of the mind; if we do have to worry about tomorrow. To prevent this, just take care of today's load. It gives us a great relief. However, I want you to read very carefully this verse: "Do not worry about tomorrow, for tomorrow will worry about its own things." Christ's meaning here is that tomorrow is dependent upon the Hand of God and He was not encouraging us to just postpone the daily tasks. He will take care of our burdens according to His Will and for our best benefit. Cicero, the Roman poet said, "If you want to live long, live slowly and walk slowly." We already have eternal life through Jesus Christ who suffered the pain of death and resurrected. We have plenty of life before us. So, we can afford to walk slowly, as if we possessed everything in the world.

Fourthly, Take care of your tasks each day. Try to avoid the expression, 'I will take care of that tomorrow." In a glance, it looked like that Christ was encouraging us to have just easy life in this sermon. But, do not misunderstand His intent. The birds in Christ's parable were not the birds that were just sitting and taking it easy in the trees. No, Christ was addressing the industrious birds, those flying in the air or those foraging for food or those taking care of their nests. When God gives us tasks, He also will give us enough ability to complete each task timely. When we complete each task timely, there will be no cause to worry about its completion in the days ahead.

In conclusion, allow me to say: Do not let worry sit in your mind, smoldering and tearing you into pieces. Remember, God, who is our Heavenly Father will take care of you! God is our strength. There is nothing that we do alone. God is always with us and He is our own personal loving Father. Seek the Lord and He will take care of you! It is our privilege to live free life from worry and anxiety.

CHAPTER 3

NEW LIFE MEANS TO HAVE A LIFE BORN ANEW IN SPIRIT.

New life means to have a reconciled life with God and the Neighbors

New life means progressively renewed everyday

New life means to have a transformed life as a whole being, spiritually and phyiscally

Jesus said that God is the "God of Abraham, Isaac, and Jacob." He also revealed Himself as Jacob's personal God: "I am Jacob's Almighty God." He is the God of living persons, a personal God of "I and Thou," not "I and it." (As the Martin Buber defines the personal relationship with God and us, not like the relation with the objective that has no feeling and thought)

Our living God creates, motivates, moves, guides, and inspires us. He leads our lives with His sovereignty. He jumps our heart, balances the seasons of the year, counts our hairs, provides our food, and protects us from harm. He is the Lord of our lives (Psalm 139:13–15; Isaiah 44:24, 64:8).

Born Anew means born again as a new creation. Jesus Christ who came to the world with the incarnation personally visits with you and changes you as a new person.

I want to introduce three people who have been experienced the amazing conversion changed as a new person when they had met Christ, God the son and God the father personally as I and Thou: Jacob, Nicodemus, and Samaritan woman and the reformer Martin Luther.

Jacob changed as a new person, Israel
Genesis 32:22-32

There is a time that we even could not pray because we are depressed deeply and grieving. But God will be with us even at that very moment closely as a mother who stays overnight with her baby when her baby groans with sickness. It is the promise of God Romans Chapter 8 says: 'The Spirit helps us in our weakness. We do not know what we ought to pray for, but the Spirit Himself intercedes for us with groans that words can't express. And he who searches our hearts know the mind of the Spirit, because the Spirit intercedes for the saints in accordance with God's will." Genesis chapter 32 showed that God hears us and intercedes our life to lead his people to the righteous way.

The summary of principle that we find in this chapter would be like this:

1. The darkness of night, the inner turmoil of our lives, is the prelude to the bright morning that would give you the peace of mind.

2. It hurts, really hurts when God deals justly with us. But, if we let Him prevail in our life, God will reward us with the bright morning of the soul. So, do not become filled with despair at the time of hardship. Look to the future with a positive attitude. God will deal mercifully with you. Let God prevail in your life. Amen

3. Real blessings come to us when we are transformed into new creatures of God. This truth echoes when Jesus said, "Blessed are the poor in spirit because the kingdom of God is theirs."

Is there a conversion experience in the Old Testament Era? That is a controversial and theological question. Conversion has two sides: one negative and one positive. First thing should happen is the recognition of sin and repentance. It is not so pleasant to go through this process, yet without this no one can experience and move toward the positive transformation and have an experience of the joy of salvation and real peace in the spirit.

The passage today is the narrative story about Jacob's mystical experience in the Jabbok stream, located in the upper part of the Jordan River. There, he encountered God in a very interesting and mystical way. This story portrays a man who was in the deep darkness because of his dilemma. It also describes a man who was struggling alone because of his inner conflicts resulting from relationships and anxiety. All through the night, he was wrestling, praying, questioning, tossing and struggling with his inner problems of sin, fear, distress and depression. It should have been a painful night for him because he thought that he was struggling all alone. However, God was struggling with him and Godly intervention enabled Jacob to face the bright morning.

This story presents itself almost like a legend of Israel, who is the ancestor of the Jews. It is similar with the story of ancient Greek legend. However, this story gives us a profound theological doctrine; a simple but very essential doctrinal issue, which is the issue of the conversion experience of one human being who was in a desperate moment. It also tells that there is a spiritual struggling, painful, and trouble-tossed dark night of a soul before one person receives spiritual blessings. It assures that the bright morning and the final victory will surely come to God's chosen and beloved children. This image gives us a sense of hope of victory in any circumstances that echoes what Romans 8:31 say, "If God is for us, who can be against us. In all these things, we are more than conquerors through Him who loves us."

Jacob's pilgrimage of life is a picture of one human being who struggles with fate and overcomes fate to achieve the final success. He was born as a second son of his family. In the middle-eastern Asian society, especially in the ancient period, position in the family meant a lot. The second son could not receive any inheritance or blessings from his parents. As a second son there was no opportunity to inherit blessings from his father. However, Jacob never gave up the blessings from his father. He did not render his life to fate and the human condition because he believed that God would help in any circumstances if he did his best. He never despaired.

However, in chapter 32 of Genesis, Jacob was in a very depressive and stressful situation. When I read Genesis Chapter 32 Verse 7 which the phrase that says, "In a great fear and distress", caught my attention. The King James Version translates the passage like this: "Jacob was greatly afraid and distressed." Modern people have many problems caused by stress. Stress can affect their lives seriously. It even could damage their health. When I read about the distress of Jacob, I was amazed to know that here was a man in the Bible who lived in an ancient time and suffered with a stress problem. Stress is, therefore, not only the problem of modern people but also a common problem of human beings at any time in history.

In psychology stress is defined as anything that threatens us, prods us, scares us, worries us, thrills us and it is anything that pushes us and gives tension. We are all under stress every day. It is necessary for us to move, think and work. The only problem is when that stress is more than we can bear with it. Now, in Jacob's situation, the tension was much more than he could handle.

Why, then, was he distressed? What was the cause of his distress? First of all, the root of the distress was Jacob's fear of death because Esau threatened Jacob's life. The passage said that Jacob was greatly afraid of his brother Esau. In returning to Cannon, Jacob knew that he would have to face Esau. Twenty years earlier Esau had vowed to kill Jacob because of Jacob's deception. As he came closer to his homeland, Jacob became more anxious because of his memory of Esau's anger. Jacob thought about the man of a hairy and strong hunter was waiting for revenge with his sharp sword. So, Jacob wanted to do all his best to pacify with his brother. Jacob sent a messenger to see what was going on in his brother's domain. When the messenger came back and reported that his brother Esau was coming to meet him with 400 strong men, Jacob thought that his brother was going to kill him and destroy his whole family.

What is fear? It is the cry of alarm raised by senses, which act as guardians of the body. When we sense danger, our organism is put in the position of defense. Fear is the natural response to danger. Without fear no organism could survive. Not only does everyone fear, but also all should fear. We sometimes misunderstand that Christianity does not allow fear. However, the Bible never condemns fear. Instead, Bible simply tells us how to overcome fear. Jacob's fear was caused by the threat of death. There is only one universal fear among all living beings and that is the fear of death. However, in a strict sense, one must be a human in order to feel it. The animal knows pain and fears it. But human beings alone are able to project themselves into the future and know the deep mystery of death, and therefore, human species suffer more than other species because of the fear of death. Human knows that death means 1) separation from loved ones and farewell forever; and 2) it means the end. To human, death is more fearful because they know that it would bring pains of the last agony. Even Jesus Christ, the Son of God was afraid of the 'last agony'. He was also deeply distressed and troubled before the crucifixion. He asked His disciple, "My soul is overwhelmed with sorrow to the point of death, so stay with me." And He prayed to God, "Abba Father, if possible, take this cup away from me."

Due to his fear of death, Jacob was depressed so much. Now, Jacob was showing significant symptoms of depression: 1) withdrawal from people and activities; 2) Loss of pleasure and enjoyment of life; 3) a feeling of sadness; 4) disappointment and loneliness; 5) a sleeping disturbance. (Verses 24, 13, 21, 22) In this stressful situation, it is difficult to find a way out. However, Jacob did three things.

First, he prayed to God in his time of crisis. Prayer is a great power source and it is our privilege. Philippians Chapter 4:4-7 says, "Rejoice in the Lord always, I will say again rejoice. Do not be anxious about anything. By prayer and petition and with thanksgiving, present your request to God. And the peace of God, which transcends all understanding, will guard your hearts and minds in Christ Jesus."

Secondly, he depended upon the promise of God (verse 12). In Jacob's prayer, Jacob not only requested his need, he also stood on the promise of God. Jacob petitioned, "Lord, you promised me that you would stay with me and protect and lead my life. Now, I need your help. So, save my life from my brother's hand according to your promise."

Most importantly of all, after the wrestling with God, Jacob recovered from his depression because God Himself came down and helped him. Now this is the story. In verses 22-24, we can find that Jacob stood all night alone. He sent his whole family and all his possessions over the stream and he stayed behind the river by alone. How awful it is to be so lonesome! Jacob was like a lonely bird left alone in the big forest at night. He was like a Psalmist who sang, "My heart is in anguish within me, the terrors of death assail me, fear and trembling have beset me, horror has overwhelmed me and I have said, 'Oh, that I had the wings of dove! I would fly away and be at rest.'" Have you ever been in a mood like this or found yourself in similar situation?

Anxiety and distress caused him to have a sleepless night. One of the worst pains is a sleeping disorder. It is not amusing at all. It surely is a torture. God gives sound sleep to those who rest in His Peace. What is the aloneness of Jacob in front of Jabbok stream telling us today?

It tells us the limitation of human wisdom and power. Jacob had a strong will power. He had never felt any task to be impossible before. However, even Jacob now faced the limitations of human beings.

It also tells us that human being have stand before God alone. This story of Jacob's aloneness in front of Jabbok River is allegorical picture of life. The Jabbok River can be as the 'river of death', 'sin', or 'human limitation' Canaan was the Promised Land to the Israelite and it could symbolize the life in God's promised heavenly realm in our current life or our home in heaven in the future. Jacob yearned to go to his homeland for twenty years, and now he was right there just few miles away. The homeland, for which he desired, was just across the small rapid stream. All of his family already cross over the Jabbok stream and was over there on the other side, yet Jacob could not cross over the stream. There were a lot of people around him, but no one knew what Jacob was going through. Furthermore, nobody could help him to cross the stream and get into his treasured land. As a Danish philosopher expressed, Jacob was like a lonely man among the crowd. All human beings must face this problem at some point of their lives because we are born alone and will go alone. This time should be a hard time, but it is a time when God can work within Jacob's life and really help him.

When Jacob stood alone in the presence of God, God Himself visited Jacob. As a result, Jacob experienced a dramatic conversion. During the lonesome, desperate night, 'a man', who approached Jacob, wrestled with him till daybreak. Imagine that you are in the situation of Jacob. It is a dark night, you are alone in the forest and the dark river is in front of you and an unknown man is approaching to you. It should be a frightening moment. But, to continue, Jacob held the waist of this unknown man and wrestles with him all night.

This picture of wrestling looks funny. Doesn't it? I cannot understand what Jacob was doing. But I know that Jacob was in desperate need. It was quite questionable who the man was. But the Scripture gives some clues. Hosea 12: 14 say, "The man was an angel. And Jacob's confession says "The man was God Himself." Jacob said, "I saw God face to face, yet my life is spared." (Verse 30) To sums up these factors, I can say that the man who wrestled with Jacob all night was God who appeared as the human form of an angel. We can call this as apparition. 'A man' could be the 'Pre-Incarnation of Jesus Christ'. Jesus Christ, as the God the Son, stayed within Jacob in the time of his desperate need. Jesus not only stayed there, but also struggled with Jacob.

Help comes from above! We sometimes do not have strength even to pray to God, yet the hands of God are always strong enough to hold our hands and escort us to the Land of Promise through the valley of death. When Jacob couldn't do anything, and faced human limitation,

God Himself came down to help him and wrestled with his problems.

What happened when God wrestled with Jacob? Two things happened to Jacob's life at that night.

First, Jacob hurt in his hip. Jacob desperately needed help and so he held the man firmly and would not let him go. When the man found that He could not overpower Jacob, the man touched the socket of Jacob's hip. Jacob's hip was misplaced and Jacob became disabled. When God deals with you, you can be hurt. Sometimes it could make you disable person temporary.

Second, Jacob's name was changed as Israel. Jacob asked the man to give him blessing. The man answered to Jacob, 'since you ask the blessing, I want to know your name. 'How do you call your name?' Jacob answered, 'I am Jacob'. Jacob means deceiver or cheater. Jacob cheated to obtain blessings at his youth age. And later, his uncle cheated Jacob for 14 years of his life. Cheating and cheated! It was his life cycle. Jacob carried the name 'cheater' all of his life. Who in the world want to carry the name cheater? God changed his name as Israel and it has two profound meanings. The first meaning is that God has changed the person. Israel is composed with two words; Ishra-EL. in the Hebrew language, Ishra is defined as a prince and EL means God. Hence, Jacob became the prince of God, Ishra-EL.

In the New Testament concept, the moment that Jacob's name changed as Israel could be a moment of 'Born-again' or 'Transformation'. He was changed as a new creature; the cheater became the prince of God. God transformed Jacob's life by grace. Changing a name does not only mean changed in a literal sense, but also a complete change of character. Indeed, it means a change in the whole human being. Jacob's real blessing was the experience of conversion as God had changed his name to Israel. In the Hebrew traditional dictionary, it gives a very detailed linguistic interpretation of Israel that could be spelled as 'Isahr-EL'. 'Isahr' means prevail and 'EL' means God. So, Second interpretation of the meaning of Israel is 'Let God prevails'. That interpretation is in tune with verse 28. Let me read this verse, "Your name will no longer be Jacob, but Israel, because you have struggled with God and with men and have overcome. The verb in verse 28, 'overcome' could be best illustrated when we compare to a father wrestling with his little son. The Father is stronger, but he just lets the son win. So, when Jacob overcame in the wrestling it was because God let him won and God hit Jacob's hip. So, actually God prevailed and overcame in Jacob's life.

The first and the second definition of the name, Israel, have some continuity. If you let God prevail in your life, you will receive the blessing of God that transforms you into a new creature, a prince of God.

After God had changed Jacob's name, Jacob became a total new being and a bright morning opened upon Jacob's life. It was the dawning of a new soul. Jacob called the place of this occurrence 'Peniel,' because he encountered God face to face and his life was spared. Peniel means 'I encountered God's face'. The passage in verse 31 describes the beautiful sunrise at the Jabbok River; "The sun rose above Jacob as he passed Peniel." It was an allegorical description of a new dawn that began for Jacob when he encountered God's face. The verse describes not only the beauty of nature in the sunrise in the Jabbok stream, but also the brightness of the grace of God that shines within the man who encountered God. Verse 31 continues, "He was limping."

As you look at the back of this man, you could see that he was hurt. He limped, was disabled and looked miserable. However, if you look directly at his face, the bright morning sunshine which was the grace of God shone upon his face. As the grace of God shone upon Jacob, the peace of God stayed with him. As God's grace shone upon Jacob's life, all his fear, anxiety and distress disappeared.

Jesus personally met with Nicodemus and gives the secret of how to be changed as a new person and born again
John 3: 1-18

II Corinthians 5:17 says, "Therefore, if anyone is in Christ, he is a new creation; the old has gone, the new has come".

Christian life is renewed and changed life. New means change. So, having a Christian life means new start with a change. With a new life, we could have a hope. We do not have to move to some distant land to begin new life. We just need to be changed inwardly.

The phrase, "To be born again" was first used by Christ. John 3:1-8 records Jesus teaches Nicodemus about the "Born Again" This phrase seems very familiar and easy to understand. However, when Christ first used this phrase, the prominent Bible scholar could not understand what is mean to be born again. He was so much embarrassed and confused.

1. Now there was a Pharisee, a man named Nicodemus who was a member of the Jewish ruling council.
2. He came to Jesus at night and said, "Rabbi, we know that you are a teacher who has come from God. For no one could perform the signs you are doing if God were not with him."
3. Jesus replied, "Very truly I tell you, no one can see the kingdom of God unless they are born again."
4. "How can someone be born when they are old?" Nicodemus asked. "Surely they cannot enter a second time into their mother's womb to be born!"
5. Jesus answered, "Very truly I tell you, no one can enter the kingdom of God unless they are born of water and the Spirit.
6. Flesh gives birth to flesh, but the Spirit gives birth to spirit.

7   You should not be surprised at my saying, 'You must be born again.'

8   The wind blows wherever it pleases. You hear its sound, but you cannot tell where it comes from or where it is going. So it is with everyone born of the Spirit."

(John 3:1-8 NIV)

Nicodemus was shocked when he heard that he have to be born again. He asked Christ," How can a man be born again when he is old?" He was saying that he could not go back to his mother's womb since he already have a physical body and even lived a long and became old. His understanding of "born again" is physically and biologically born as a new baby. To us, it is so interesting to hear this prominent Old testament scholar could never have a clue what Jesus was saying spiritually born again.

Jesus explains very kindly the simple truth that Spirit of God helps us to be born again and transformed as a new person at verses 5-8.

5   esus answered, "Very truly I tell you, no one can enter the kingdom of God unless they are born of water and the Spirit.

6   6 Flesh gives birth to flesh, but the Spirit gives birth to spirit.

7   You should not be surprised at my saying, 'You must be born again.'

8   The wind blows wherever it pleases. You hear its sound, but you cannot tell where it comes from or where it is going. So it is with everyone born of the Spirit."

Spirit/Flesh!

Jesus clearly distinguished between Spirit and flesh. Jesus says, "Flesh gives birth to flesh and the Spirit gives birth to spirit." 1st Corinthians 15:50 says, "I declare to you, brother, that flesh and blood cannot inherit the kingdom of God, nor the perishable inherit the imperishable."

Now, let me briefly tell you how we can be born again more precisely.

As Jesus said, "born of water and the Spirit"

Two things Jesus said, 1) Born of water 2) Spirit.

What does it mean to be born of water?

I want to introduce what "Life Change" interpretation of "born of water".

1) Water represents repentance and purification, as in John the Baptist's Baptism 2) Water represents natural procreation-human semen. 3) Water represents spiritual procreation. 4) Water refers to Christian's baptism. [2]

Baptism of John the Baptist was done when people confesses their sin and do the repentance. So, Born of water means realizing human fault and weakness and sinfulness and repent and express their desire to become purified by water baptism.

However, water baptism is not enough to become a born again Christian.

People need the divine inspiration of the Holy Spirit powerfully working in their soul and the spirit and the heart. Spirit come down when people understand God's redemptive love through Christ's sacrificial suffering, death and the resurrection.

The famous word, the theme scripture of the Bible, John 3:16 that is the core of the gospel of Christ suffering on the cross and the resurrection to give us way the get eternal life was the first given to Nicodemus. So, as Nicodemus understand John 3:16, he could experience the Spirit of God coming to his heart and be born again. (John 3:10-20)

---

[2]   A Life-changing encounter with God's Word from the book of John, Navigators, NAVEPRESS, USA, 1987, page 51.

Now, let me summarize simple way how people can be born again, born a new from above. Realize how sinful they are, truly repent and understand God's redemptive love of forgiving, and accept Christ as their savior who would give salvation and the eternal life.

For this understanding Jesus spends a lot a time with Nicodemus personally to explain the gospel. For your better understanding, I would like to talk two subjects: 1) God's truly love 2) True Forgiveness and Fatherly love to the prodigal son.

Truthful Love
John 3:16

John 3:16 best explains how much God loved humankind. It says that God so much loved humankind that He gave His one and only begotten Son Jesus Christ to save humankind from sin, death, and fiery eternal judgment.

Therefore, first, true love is sacrificing. God expressed His true love toward us with the sacrifice of His Son.

One day a child asked her Sunday school teacher, "Teacher, how much does God love us?" The teacher opened his arms, stretched them wide, and said, "This much, and He died for you on the cross like this to show His love to you." That is what Jesus did to show you how much God loves you. Jesus came to this world as a king of kings. However, He was a savior king who suffered to redeem us and became a ransom for all of us.

There was a small aircraft crash once. The emergency team arrived to save the pilot and the passengers. However, when they arrived, they thought there could be no survivors with that hard of a crash. Everything smelled like burning already. Everything became ashes and smog. Yet they heard one baby crying in the midst of the smog. When the emergency medic team reached near the smog, they found one mother protectively embracing a baby. The mother died, and the baby survived. This baby was the only survivor when the aircraft clashed, because of the mother's sacrificial love.

It may be easy just to say, "I love you." However, true love should accompany sacrifice, commitment, and effort toward the beloved. True love brings pain.

Mother Teresa, who was awarded the Nobel Peace Prize in 1980 said, "True love hurts." She continued, "It hurt God when He gave His only begotten Son to the world; it hurt Jesus when He died on the cross; it hurt His Mother, Mary, to see her precious Son suffering on the cross."

Christ showed His sacrificial love on the cross. Christ suffered on the cross for us. Definitely, it was not because of His sin, it was for our redemption. But people responded differently. When Jesus hung on the cross, there were two criminals hung on each side. One of the criminals screamed and hurled insults at Christ, saying, "Aren't you the Christ? Then, save yourself and us."

Christ cried with a loud voice in His extreme suffering: "Eloi, Eloi, lama sabachthani," which means, "My God, my God, why have you forsaken Me?" Hearing this, some people ridiculed Him: "Leave Him alone. Let's see if Elijah comes to save Him." However, some people who witnessed Christ's suffering and death on the cross realized Christ was their Messiah. One centurion and some other Roman guardians, seeing all the events that happened, exclaimed, "Surely, He was the Son of God!" And the criminal who hung with Christ on the other side rebuked the one who ridiculed Christ, "Don't you fear God? We are punished justly, for we are getting what our deeds deserve. But this man has done nothing wrong." He asked Jesus, "Jesus, remember me when you come into your kingdom." Jesus answered him, "I tell you the truth, today you will be with Me in paradise." On the cross in His extreme pain, Jesus gave hope to the one who was dying hopelessly and carried him to paradise. Jesus took all our sins, sorrows, and pains. He redeemed us. How could Jesus could show such genuine love and care for a hopeless person at the moment of His deep suffering and hurt? This shows Christ's sacrificial love for humankind.

Second, after sacrifice, true love is accepting others instead of rejecting them. One of humankind's deepest desires is the yearning for belonging. In Daniel Defoe's famous novel Robinson Crusoe, Crusoe experienced the hurt in human society and wanted to escape from people. He chose to live alone on an isolated island. However, he discovered one Friday that he should come back to society even though there still were conflicts in his relationships with others. Human beings need to belong to a group of people. Otherwise, they are too lonely to survive. At the same time, there is always hurt when people gather.

Live alone, or belong to society?

That is the question! That is the dilemma!

The answer would be to make an accepting society whose members could get along well and be happy together as they built up good relationships. The key is to love by accepting each other. That was the love that Jesus Christ showed. It was the love that God showed (Luke 15). Jesus accepted all: the lepers, the prostitutes, people who were born blind, uneducated people, fishermen, robbers, poor people, rich people, outcast people, and novel people as well.

How come people cannot accept each other? It could be because of their differences, pride, jealousy, and so on. The biggest reason could be zealousness. Rejection is the absence of compassion and the overflowing of zealousness. Joseph was the most beloved son among Jacob's sons. Jacob gave him the best clothes and showed his favor to Joseph. Jacob's showing favoritism was not wise. Yet the more serious problem was the zealousness with which Joseph's brothers turned on him. They rejected him as their blood, and their zealous response blinded them so that they could put their own blood in a dungeon, which should have killed him. With their zealous competitiveness, they caused their brother great misery. If they had just accepted Joseph as their brother and had been compassionate toward him, they would have loved him as the charming youngest.

Be merciful, be compassionate, and accept each other with the compassion of God. That is the love that Jesus showed us. Human beings are all like dust; no one could ever be perfect and blameless. So, all human beings are the object of His mercy, not competition. Psalm 103:13–14 says, "As a father has compassion on his children, so the Lord has compassion on those who fear him; for he knows how we are formed, he remembers that we are dust."

If we accepted each other with God's compassion, we would make a happy, holy city in this world like the one described in Isaiah 11:6–9: "The wolf will live with the lamb, the leopard will lie down with the goat, the calf and the lion and the yearling together; and a little child will lead them. The cow will feed with the bear, their young will lie together, and the lion will eat straw like the ox. The infant will play near the hole of the cobra, and the young child put his hand into the viper's nest. They will neither harm nor destroy on my entire holy mountain, for the earth will be full of the knowledge of the Lord."

Acceptance is best described in the novel Les Miserables. One priest's forgiveness and acceptance of Jean Valjean changed him into an honorable man. The priest's accepting this man as God's child changed his heart and Jean Valjean became a marvelous Christian. It was the same love that Jesus showed us. Jesus accepted the robber as His child and said, "You are with Me today in paradise." Christ will accept you as you are with His compassionate love.

I pray that God helps you realize how much He loves you by showing you His sacrifice and how He accepts you. I pray that God helps you to love each other with a sacrificial and accepting love.

For Reflection and Discussion

1. What do you do when you love someone? Think about those who sacrifice their lives for your wellness, health, and happiness. Discuss the first aspect of love, which is sacrifice.

2. Meditate on Jesus, who, in His time of suffering, gave the hope of eternal life to the man who was dying on the cross. Discuss the sacrificial love of Jesus Christ. Meditate on Psalm 103:13–14 and John 3:16, and think about Jesus Christ's sacrificial love for you.

3. Discuss the second aspect of love, which is acceptance. What are reasons why people cannot always accept each other? Think about Jesus, who accepts all people as children of God regardless of their backgrounds.

True Forgiveness and Fatherly love to the prodigal son
Luke 15, Matthew 18:11–13

There was a group of religious people who were segregated, especially outcast, and did not associate with any people who did not meet their standards. Their religious sect was the Pharisees. They were against Jesus because Jesus wanted to reach out to the outcast in His day. Luke 15 recounts three parables that Jesus shared in the context of the Pharisees' opposition and grumbling about Him associating with sinners (Luke 14:1, 5:30, 7:39).

Jesus gave three parallel parables about a lost coin, lost sheep, and lost son to teach that we should understand God's love for the lost and rejoice in finding the lost.

The real targeted audience of these parables was actually the Pharisees, who were described as those who worked hard and behaved decently and yet were reluctant to welcome the returned brother. Jesus' purpose of telling this parable was not to be judgmental but to help those people who never could grasp the meaning of grace to understand the heart of God, the Father, who is compassionate to the lost. Jesus also wanted them to have the privilege to experience real joy and join in the great work of God's redemption.

Three parables in Luke 15 speak of the same theme: God is seeking the lost and is joyful when he finds the lost. The first two parables are about a shepherd looking for the one lost sheep and a lady looking for a lost coin. The lost sheep and the lost coin signify the lost people, the sinners of those days. The third parable is about the father who is reunited with his prodigal son; two parables are about seeking and one is about waiting. I want you to see the connection between waiting and searching: waiting is strong expression of the love of the one who is seeking. The Lord was seeking and then waiting and again seeking for lost souls. God's unconditional love for lost people is well expressed in these parables, which amazingly illustrate God's love in three ways.

First, he was lost and now is found.

In the parable of the prodigal son, the father tried to persuade his first son that they had to accept the other son who came back after doing despicable things: "We had to celebrate and be glad, because this brother of yours was dead and is alive again; he was lost and is found" (Luke 15:31).

Human beings are lost. The Lord has been seeking and then waiting and again seeking the lost souls from the time when Adam and Eve were lost in the garden of Eden; "The Lord God called to the man, 'Where are you?'" (Genesis 3:9). From the time when Adam and Eve sinned and hid themselves from God, they were lost beings. From the time when the prodigal son left his father's house and lost his relationship with the father, he was lost. People are lost when they do not know the love of God and have lost their relationship with God.

Lost in Greek, is apollumi, which describes a thing that is not used or claimed; it refers to something no longer visible, known, possessed, or attainable. A lost person is one who is unable to find the way, confused, helpless, ruined, or destroyed physically, mentally, or morally. Lostness in the spiritual world goes little further than the literal meaning. It means anyone who is out of touch with the love of the eternal God. Lostness means separation, isolation, and alienation, being cut off from our true existence. One of the greatest evangelists in these recent centuries, D. L. Moody said, "I see every person as though he had a large L in the midst of his forehead. I consider him lost until I know he is saved."

Ernest Hemingway, who wrote "The Old man and the Sea," described an old man who caught a whale while fishing in his ragged, small fishing boat. He pulled the big whale as he fought against the waves of the outraged sea. The old man struggled to bring the whale to land. Although a shark attacked him on the way, he kept the whale successfully. Finally, he arrived on land and pulled out the whale. However, the only thing he could see was the whale's skeleton; the shark had eaten it all on the way.

Hemingway, although he was a famous and respected writer, shot himself in his head and killed himself. He was like Adam hiding behind the fig leaves, lost. People are lost if they are out of touch with the eternity and true love of God.

However, the good news is that God is desperately waiting for His children to come back and is looking for them like a tearful mother who lost her young boy.

God still remembers people who are lost and wants to find them. He feels a great sense of loss when His children are lost and do not come back to Him, as described in this parable of the lost son. The lost coin could be one of ten held together by a silver chain and worn on a headpiece to signify a woman was married. No one might have cared about the lost coin, as it did not have a lot of value, yet it was so valuable for this young married lady. Nobody cared about the prodigal son, because he was a despicable boy; maybe he got drunk all the time and associated with prostitutes. However, to his father, he was a dear son created in his own image. The image of the father's face, foot, and all spiritual, mental, and physical DNA were ingrained in this son—although some of it had faded because of the son's sinful life.

Second, there is joy in finding the lost.

Hole in one!

I could never forget the joy of the occasion when I played golf and hit a hole in one! It rolled somewhere, and I thought that it had gone off the green. I remember wondering, "Where is the ball? I cannot find it anywhere." I looked at everywhere! One of my friends said, "It is right here inside the hole. It rolled slowly and all of sudden disappeared. It was in the hole." Do you know how joyful it was to find the ball I thought I'd lost was in the hole?

The joy of the father was much more than that. Luke 15:20–22 reads:

But while he was still a long way off, his father saw him and was filled with compassion for him; he ran to his son, threw his arms around him and kissed him. The son said to him, "Father, I have sinned against heaven and against you. I am no longer worthy to be called your son." But the father said to his servants, "Quick! Bring the best robe and put it on him. Put a ring on his finger and sandals on his feet. Bring the fattened calf and kill it. Let's have a feast and celebrate. For this son of mine was dead and is alive again; he was lost and found."

That was Jesus' joy when He was with sinners, tax collectors, prostitutes, outcast laborers, fishers, and zealots. He seemed not to be as pious as religious leader should be; rather, He spent time with a gaggle of outcasts. It reminded people of David, who joyfully danced without any skirts when he got God's lost ark back. Even his royal wife despised David at that time. The joyful father accepted and welcomed his formerly lost and prodigal son with a joyful heart; they shared tears and laughter together!

Jesus emphasized the clergyman's role in finding lost human beings in Matthew 18:10–13.

The New International Version (NIV) of Matthew 18:10–14 reads:

See that you do not despise one of these little ones. For I tell you that their angels in heaven always see the face of my Father in heaven. [No verse 11.] What do you think? If a man owns a hundred sheep, and one of them wanders away, will he not leave the ninety-nine on the hills and go to look for the one that wandered off? And if he finds it, truly I tell you, he is happier about that one sheep than about the ninety-nine that did not wander off. In the same way your Father in heaven is not willing that any of these little ones should perish.

Many Bible versions of Matthew 18 leave out verse 11 as in this excerpt. But the King James Version includes verse 11, which reads; "For the Son of man is come to save that which was lost." Although Matthew 18:11 is not found in the earliest and best manuscripts, it may have been encouraged by the words of Luke 19:10 and added by a later scribe to provide a better bridge between Matthew 18:10 and the parable in Matthew 18:12–14. It is generally believed that the context of Luke 19:10 is Luke 18, which describes Jesus accepting Zacchaeus, whom had a high social status and whom everyone despised. However, it is safer to say that Matthew 18:11, which discusses the lostness of human beings, comes from the concept of Luke 15, which explains the father's unconditional love for his lost son.

The disciples, future spiritual leaders, learned from Jesus that they had to love the lost and people with low social statuses (Matthew 18:1–10). Matthew understood the human condition of lostness and God's heart toward the lost people to find them because of his personal experience and he described best it in Matthew 18:14: "Your heavenly Father do not want any of these little one to be lost." (author's paraphrase)

There was an occasion when the disciples asked the question, "Who is the greatest in the kingdom of heaven?" To answer, Jesus held a little child and said, "I tell you the truth, unless you change and become like little children, you will never enter the kingdom of heaven" (Matthew 18:1–3). Little children, people of low social status, and the poor were not welcome to society in Jesus' day—just like these days. Children sometimes were ignored and even not included in the count of family members. That was the context for Jesus' parable of the lost sheep.

Therefore, lost people could be people who are ignored and of low social status. Jesus said, "See that you do not despise one of these little ones. For I tell you that their angels in heaven always see the face of my Father in heaven" (Matthew 18:10).

Matthew included social embracement with spirituality. In verse 10, Matthew says that we should not ignore people of low social status. It is amazing to hear that even little ones have their designated angels who report to God the Father directly on how they are treated. Jesus reminds those who look down on people with low income or low social status that we all have our own angels to report to God in heaven on how we were treated.

Third, pardon, grace, welcome, and privilege.

The prodigal son did not expect to be pardoned. However, grace was given to him. Why? The father says, "For this son of mine was dead and is alive again; he was lost and is found. So, let us celebrate." The only condition for this forgiveness was that the father and son had a relationship. The father welcomed his son home and rejoiced just because his son was his own; it was his son, his life and blood.

The father's grace was expressed in three ways.

- Robe: This was not just a regular robe; it was the best robe that was reserved for notable guests. The returned son was a notable guest.

- Ring: By giving his son a ring, the father accepted him as his own, forgot what he had done, forgave all, and took him back.

- Sandals: Sandals were a luxury in those days; they were not for servants but for sons. Therefore, this gift signifies the father's full acceptance of his returned son.

The returned son did not deserve to get all of those nice gifts. The lost son was not significant enough to get this attention from his father. However, it was given by the grace of God. Just like the silver coin, the lost sheep, and the prodigal son, you may not be significant to others. But, you are significantly important to God, the Father. Therefore, God will be extremely joyful when He gets you back if you are lost. My prayer is that I could embrace the lost people in my ministry and look for them to return to God with the shepherd's heart and the father's broken heart. It is my prayer that today's ministers would have Jesus' shepherd heart for the lost people, outcasts, and sinners.

For Reflection and Discussion

1. Have you experienced the loss of something or someone valuable in your personal life? If you did, share your experience with the group.

2. Who are today's lost people?

3. Meditate on and discuss the father who was waiting for his lost son and joyfully welcomed him back home.

4. How do you treat the outcast or someone who has a lower social status than you?

5. What can you do to minister to lost people?

6. Meditate on Luke 15:20–24 and discuss what was unexpected about the father's welcoming of the prodigal son. What does this express about God's love for you?

BOOK 5: NEW LIFE

Jesus met Samaritan women personally and changed her life as a new person
John chapter 4

Now, I would like to tell you the story of the Samaritan woman and Jesus. It is one of the most famous stories in the Bible. I believe that you have often heard this story. It begins in John's gospel chapter four. Now, Jesus was walking and had long journey going through Samaria, the hot desert. He was thirsty and hungry. Soon He arrived to a town in Samaria called Sychar, where there was Jacob's well. (Joseph inherited this well) Jesus was so tired that he just sat down by the well. And it was about the sixth hour; it is around noontime in our measurement of time. Jesus was so thirsty. He asked the Samaritan woman, "Will you give me a drink?" The Samaritan woman said to Jesus very unkindly, "You are a Jew and I am a Samaritan woman. How can you ask me for a drink?" She was very unkind because Jews never associated with Samaritans. Jesus answered her, "If you knew the gift of God and who it is that asks you for a drink, you would have asked Him and He would have given you living water." Jesus is the Creator, His nationality was Jewish, His gender was man. This woman was Samaritan, a human and a woman. There are many differences here. However, Jesus and the Samaritan woman had one common need. Both needed something to quench their thirst – Jesus needs water to quench his thirsty - this woman, spiritually. As a response for Jesus' asking for water, this woman who always came to the well of Jacob, now asked Jesus one question, "Are you greater than our father, Jacob?"

Isaiah said, "Why spend money on what is not bread and expend your labor on what does not satisfy? (Isaiah 55:2) Success in one's career, personal achievement, economical stability, recognition, friendship, and a happy marriage! We value all of those physical and emotional desires and it is important to have those desires. However, as we have experienced, we get an "empty feeling" even after we obtain those things that we really wanted. We climb the mountain to reach our goals and successes. We thought that we would be perfectly happy once we had achieved those goals. But, that satisfaction does not last long. We should go further, succeed more and achieve more to quench our thirst for personal gain. It is like drinking salty water. The more you drink, the less your thirst is quenched.

I sometimes wondered, "Why can't humans be perfectly satisfied?" The answer is; that is how we are created. God made us to depend on Him for our spirituality, our eternity. As the book of Ecclesiastes said, "God has set eternity in the hearts of humankind." When were born, it was God that put the desire, the yearning for eternity in our conscious and in our subconscious. Only God, who is eternal, can quench our thirst for eternity. Jesus said, "Whoever drinks this water will be thirsty again, but whoever drinks the water I give him will never thirst. Indeed, the water I give him will become a spring of water welling up to eternal life." (John 4:13-14)

What does this mean? Why does the water that Jesus gives become a spring of water welling up to eternal life?

It means first that Christ's love is perfect, spiritual, eternal. So, Christ's love is spiritual drink for us. Human needs sincere and everlasting love. When the Samaritan woman heard about the spring of water welling up to eternal life, she asked Christ, "Sir, give me this water, so that I won't get thirsty again." Jesus told her, "Go, call your husband and come back." She replied, "I have no husband." Jesus said to her, "you are right when you say you have no husband. The fact is, you have had five husbands, and the man you now have is not your husband. What you have said is quite true" Either the woman was unfaithful or the husbands were unfaithful. Whatever the case, this woman had lots of experience with broken marriage. As a result, she had experienced much hurt. Whenever she drew water from Jacob's well, she thought about the story of Jacob who was sincere and faithful man Jacob, who loved only one woman.

Jacob was admirable because Jacob's love was sincere and faithful. This is another facet of the Samaritan woman's question to Christ, "Are you greater than Jacob? With this question, she was actually asking, "Is your love, God's love, more sincere and more faithful than Jacob's love for Rachel?" As Christ' love quenches the spirit of this woman, His love, Agape love will quench our thirst for the eternity.

Second meaning of what Jesus saying, "I will give you springs of water welling up to eternal" is that Christ will give us perfect sense of belongingness. Jesus was saying that God welcomed the

Samaritan woman who was rejected even by her tribes and accepting her as God's loving children. To the Samaritan woman, Jacob's well was not just a place to draw water; it was more than a physical well. This woman was looking for a sense of belongingness at Jacob's well. Think about why she was asking the unusual question, "Are you greater than our father, Jacob? She emphasized the fact that Jacob was her ancestor and she was one of the children of Jacob. And she noted that Jacob, himself, drank from the same well, as did his sons and his flocks and his herds as well. She also stated that Jacob handed over the well to her people, the Samaritans.

Have you experienced rejection from others of the same race? Have you been excluded from their association and their fellowship even you live within their neighborhood? Have you been ignored because of your differences in comparison to them? Or have you excluded others who want to associate with you? " Exclusion causes a terrible, pitiful feeling. That was just what the Samaritan woman felt. She felt ostracized, excluded and alone. Do you feel ostracized, excluded even from Christian?

However, Christ will give eternal life to us. We will not be bound by time when we join with His eternity. When we pass from this life, we will continue in that right path forever in eternity. We will not be bound by time. We will be living a spiritual life now and forever.

The Reformer Martin Luther's experience of born anew

If Abraham was justified by works, he had something to boast about—but not before God. What does Scripture say? 'Abraham believed God, and it was credited to him as righteousness.'" That is the truth that God illuminated to the hearts of Paul and Martin Luther. The Holy Spirit inspired them with of the idea, "The righteous shall live by faith."

God gives us righteousness not because He wants to degrade the ethical or moral aspects of life, but because God knows that human beings could never reach the standard of His righteousness. "For all have sinned and fall short of the glory of God, and all are justified freely by his grace through the redemption that came by Christ Jesus" (Romans 3:23–24).

Martin Luther, who was born in 1483, tried hard to become a righteous person in the dark ages of Christianity, and he became a monk. One of ways that people in his day thought they could become righteous was through self-discipline and self-restriction; they could overcome their sinful desires by climbing up Pilate's stairs in the cathedral in Rome with bare feet and bare knees. He thought that he could become free from sin by condemning the sinful body, yet as he tried harder to punish his sinfulness, he became more desperate. In response to Luther's honest and long quest, God gave a surprising answer to Luther. One day the Spirit gave him an illumination with the words of Romans 1:17: "The righteous shall live by faith":

"Luther came to the conclusion that the "justice of God" does not refer, as he had been taught, to the punishment of sinners. It means rather that the "justice" or "righteousness" of the righteous is not their own, but God's. The righteousness of God is that which is given to those who live by faith. It is given, not because they are righteous, nor because they fulfill the demands of divine justice, but simply because God wishes to give it. Luther tells us, "I felt that I had been born anew and that the gates of heaven had been opened. The phrase 'the justice of God' no longer filled me with hatred, but rather became unspeakably sweet by virtue of a great love."i1

CHAPTER 4

PERSPECTIVE THAT LEADS TO NEW LIFE

In this chapter, I want to talk about the perspectives that would lead us to have a new life. Psalms 1:1-3 says, "Blessed is the man who delights meditating the word of God day and night. He is like a tree planted by streams of water, which yields its fruit in season." The word of God gives us a new perspective of life and it leads us to have a great new life; hopeless person will change to be a hopeful person, and sick person will be changed to a healthy person. As a result, they will have a fruitful life like a tree planted by streams of water.

1. Sympathy and Understanding
2. Holy Spirit that break the barrier
3. The City of Refuge
4. The door is wide open
5. God's compassion
6. God's true love
7. God expresses love in three ways
8. Redeemed life of Ruth

Christ Understand and Sympathize
Hebrew 4:14-16

Two important nature of Jesus who make us able to approach to God boldly to receive the grace are: 1) Christ was a Human who had gone through all temptations that we go through daily 2) Christ had no sin at all.

John 1:1-4. John 1:1 states the full deity of Christ that reads as, "In the beginning was the Word, and the Word was with God, and the Word was God. He was with God in the beginning." Why is this so important for us? It is important because if Christ is not God, His death on the cross would have had nothing to do with our salvation. Many people views Christ was the one who died righteously. If Christ died on the cross just as a regular righteous man, His death would not be able gives us the redemption from our sin. Because He was Almighty God, His death became atonement for our sins. Because He w is a perfect God, Christ is able to save us. Since Christ has the almighty power and fullness of God's divinity, He has the ability to save us.

A few years ago, there was a movie entitled, "The Last Temptation of Christ', which aroused a controversial sensation to many people. I think it made a controversial sensation because people were curious about the nature of Christ's humanity. Unfortunately, there are some people who want attempt to degrade the position of Christ and just emphasize the human aspect of Christ's nature.

Throughout Christian history, the nature of Jesus Christ has been one of the most controversial issues. It is very important issue because understanding Christ's nature is directly related to our salvation. Christ Himself concerned very much about people's understanding of His nature. So, He asked two questions, "Who do people say that I am?" and "Who do you say that I am?"

Some denies 'the full deity of Christ' by saying that Jesus is only a super man who possessed unusual power. They believe that Christ is primarily a man. Some Christians gave more credit to Christ humanness by saying that "Christ is definitely a God; we agree to His deity. But, Christ is a created God, not the eternal God." What would you say about this comment?

The Nicene Creed established in A.D. 313, it proclaimed that Christ has same essence with God, the Father and God, and the Holy Spirit. The Creed said, "The Three are One and inseparable, three Persons in One Divinity. Jesus is not like God. Jesus is God."

It is very important to understand fully that Christ' essence is the same with God the Father: the very same, not just similar to God. Without our confirmation of this matter, we cannot reach the fullness of salvation. I would like to give some scripture foundation for this reasoning. Hebrew 1: 1-5 said that Christ is the exact radiance of God, the Father in His essence; not like God, But God!

Another aspect of Christ is His human aspect, which was portrayed even in the Old Testament. Isaiah 53:2-3 describes Christ as a suffering Lord and said, "He is like a root out of the ground. He had no beauty or majesty to attract us to him, nothing in his appearance that we should desire him, he was despised and rejected by men, a man of sorrow and familiar with suffering." All four Gospels also fully depict Christ as a man who has all the emotions and needs of regular human being.

- He felt hungry when he had no food.
- He wept when His beloved friend died.
- He felt tired when he had long journey in the desert.
- He was thirsty.
- He experienced the pain when Romans crucified him.
- Lastly, He was tempted just as we are.

Today's Scripture Hebrew 4:15 says, "For we have not a high priest who is unable to sympathize with our weakness, because He was in all points tempted like as we are, yet without sin" It is very important to understand that 'Christ has been tempted in every way just as we are, but was without sin' Why is the fact that Christ was tempted so important to us? Are we trying to tear down the goodness of the human Jesus? Does it make us feel better in our fallibility to know that Jesus had faults? No! Not at all! The fact that Jesus became human and experienced the temptation tells us firmly that He had been through already what we go through each day and it enabled Him to understand us. He knows how we feel emotionally physically and spiritually when we are going through temptation and trial.

Since Christ is God, He did not have to go through all of His trials. He could have chosen not to suffer. Then, why did He choose to suffer? It was because He wanted to have the ability to understand us. Hebrews Chapter 4, verse15 in NIV (New International Version) reads, "For we have not a high priest who is unable to sympathize with our weaknesses, but we have one who has been tempted in every way, just as we are-yet without sin" What does this mean? This verse means that Christ, the High Priest, surely gone through all our temptation and trials to experience suffering of human beings and share that same experience.

The word sympathizes is composed of two words: Sym+ Phathize.

Sym which means "with".

Phatos which means "experience suffering either physically or emotionally. So, the word 'sympathize' means sharing the same experience, the same suffering and same human feelings with all other human being. The Maccabees, ancient Israel' patriots, ascertained that, "To have the best view of others, one must go through the actual experience of others." There is an American Indian proverb that echoes with Maccabean' proverb which said, "To understand others, you have to the experience of walking one day in another's moccasins."

Christ is able to understand us because He had gone through all the possible sufferings and trials that we encounter in our lives. Apostle

Paul said that one of the benefits of suffering is that he/she who had suffered can really understands others and has ability to comfort those people who are going through the same problem. Paul said, "Praise be to God and the Father of our Lord Jesus Christ, the Father of compassion and the God of comfort who comforts us in all troubles, so that we can comfort those in any trouble with the comfort we ourselves have received from God. For just as the suffering of Christ flow over into our lives, so also through Christ our comfort overflows. " (2nd Corinthians 1: 3-5) Christ understands the life in the streets of Judea, the life of the outcasts, and the suffering of the sick people. We are tempted so many occasions because of weakness and frailty of human being. However, we do not despair because we have a High Priest who is able to understand us.

With the fact that our Lord has full ability of sympathy and understanding, Hebrews scripture recommends us today, "Therefore, let us approach the throne of grace with confidence so that we may receive mercy and find grace to help us in our time of need."(NIV) King James Version translates liked the following, "Let us therefore come boldly unto the throne of grace that we may obtain mercy, and find grace to help in time of need."

The throne of our God is not the throne of judgment, but the throne of grace and the throne of mercy. If we approach His throne with the confidence of His love and mercy, knowing that 'He would not reject us and would not condemn us, He will not even judge us according to our incapability'. He even would not ask us, "How couldn't you follow those simple rules and then fail?" Instead, God would accept us as we are because he understands that we human beings are from dust and fragile. Knowing that He understand us, we would be able to approach to Him comfortably.

As the father of the prodigal son who ran to accept and welcome back his son, our Lord Jesus Christ touched and cured the women who had 12 years of incurable disease. He accepted the man who was in his desperate moment of capital punishment on the cross. This Jesus would give us same mercy and grace in our time of need.

As a summary, I want you to remind you three things. First, Our Lord Christ has gone through the exact trials that you are experiencing. Second, our Lord, who now sits at the right hand of God, sympathizes with you right now. He understands you. Third, Christ is with God' throne to give you mercy and grace. Jesus is there to be your help, and therefore, give all your burdens, sorrows and worries to Him. Let us approach to God with confidence in time of our need.

The Spit breaks the barrier: By the Spirit of God Acts Chapter 2

Why did the Holy Spirit work powerfully on that particular day of Pentecost? There were two reasons why Holy Spirit worked dynamically on the day of Pentecost.

First of all, God wanted everybody to have opportunity to listen the gospel message. Jews in old days were scattered all around the world, we call it as 'Diaspora'. Although they lived in foreign countries, they had a strong sense of belonging to the Jew. Just like we traveled to visit our families on Christmas season, the Jews who lived outside of the Palestine areas traveled to Jerusalem as they went pilgrimage around the season of the Jewish religious feasts. The feast started from the Passover and continued to the spring time with other combined feasts. One of those feasts was Pentecostal feast. Pentecost is a Greek word and it means 50th, so the Pentecostal day was the fiftieth days after the Passover.

The dispersed Israelites customarily waited until the day of Pentecost either to get in to Jerusalem or go back to their home in other country because the weather conditions in the Palestine area in those days were very dangerous to travel. Those people who already stayed in Jerusalem waited to participate in the Pentecostal feast. They planned to depart to their home after the Pentecostal day was over. Even the people who were outside the Palestine came into Jerusalem on Pentecostal days. Those customarily can be found even in the Paul's travel plan at Ephesus. Paul waited at Ephesians church before he visited the Jerusalem church until few days before the Pentecostal days for the same reason. So, on the Pentecostal day, the Jerusalem was filled with the people from all around the world. God had poured His Spirit on that day because He wanted everyone to have the opportunity to listen the Gospel message. On that day, people around the world witnessed the work of Holy Spirit and they all had opportunity to listen the Gospel message. It was God's strategy for pouring His Spirit in this special occasion. What a depth of God's wisdom!

Secondly, it was the day God gave them Ten Commandment through Moses. There is symbolic meaning in the fact that the Holy Spirit worked on the day of Pentecost. Let me tell you briefly what the Pentecostal day in Old Testament days was like. Pentecostal feast is like a thanksgiving day for us. After they have harvest, they bring offering to altar, and they thanks God for His provision. They celebrate the day as blessed day and take as Holiday.

On the Passover, the Israelites got the freedom from the Egyptians and they had marched to the Promised Land. After 50 days on the march to the promise land, when it became the Pentecostal day, Moses received the Ten Commandment on the Mount of Sinai. So, they celebrated the Pentecostal day as the day when they received the word of God. What does it tells us? It tells us that Holy Spirit works dynamically when people give thanks to God. It also tells us that the Holy Spirit works when people accept the word of God.

Then, what happened when the Holy Spirit worked dynamically?

- They were able to communicate.
- They were able to understand each other.
- They were able to talk friendly with each other.

When the fire of Spirit was distributed to the believers, they began to speak in other tongues. Let us assume that we are all in international organization like European Union or NATO (North Atlantic Treaty Organization or United Nation to discuss international issues. French, German, Finland, Belgium, and all other international delegations gathered for the discussion. However, there are no linguists and no ear plug to hear the translation. All the representatives of nations could speak only their country languages. Could they communicate and discuss the issues?

In Jerusalem temple, there were Jews from every country. Since dispersion, they had settled in other countries, they had learned all other languages and their first languages were not any more Hebrews, because the majority of them were born and grew in other countries just like the 2nd/ 3rd generations of immigrants. So, it was hard for them to communicate with each other.

But when the believers who received the Holy Spirit, they started to speak in tongues. They spoke in other languages as if they were speaking those as their native languages. So, people from all around the country were able to understand exactly what they were talking about. They were all amazed and wondered and said, "How could the Galileans speak all foreign languages so fluently? They had not gone to school of foreign languages. How is it that we hear, each of our own languages?" I had very sweet congregation when I first started the ministry. When I was still in Divinity school, I had chance to minister to Multi-ethnic group; their native language was English. One day I preached that 'Since we are in Christ, we will be heir of God's kingdom'. After I preached, one of the church members approached to me and said, 'your sermon is great, but next time when you say, 'heir' pronounce 'eir' because h is silent. She did not intend to embarrass me and I knew that. Anyway, what is the language for? It is for the communication. With the composed words, we communicate our feelings, thoughts and exchange those in the dialogue.

Long time ago, before the event of falling of Babel tower, all the people on the world used one same language. When humankind started to civilize, they attempted to reach to God's level and built the tower of Babel. They said, "Let us reach to the top of heaven". Their pride made them spiritually blind and ignored God of heaven. So, God disturbed their language and made them speak all other languages. Suddenly, when one man asked for the brick, the other man understood as wood and gave him wood. They could not communicate. So, they could not work together and finally they scattered around the world. Genesis tells us that human kind started to develop languages of each country from that time on. It made hard to all of us because we have spend lots of times to study foreign languages. The followings are the processes when Babel tower fell.

- Human pride
- Get away from God- Attempt to be same with God
- Speak other languages
- Miscommunication
- Misunderstand
- Division & Conflicts
- Scatter
- War/Fighting

However, now in Acts, when the Spirit worked, they could communicate well because Spirit enables them to speak other native languages. The principle in here is not just a skill of language. The principle in here is, "When the Holy Spirit works, the barriers and conflicts between people will disappear. When Spirit works, people will be able to understand each other well enough.

What is the problem in the world nowadays? Why are there bloody wars in many parts of the world these days? Why are there so many conflicts in the families and the marriages in these days? It is because they could not communicate well enough to understand with each other. However, as we had seen in the Holy Spirit pouring event in Acts, when Spirit works, we will be able to speak in others languages and will be able to understand and love each other. So, Let us pray that God would fill us with His Spirit so that we would communicate, understand, and love each other. Holy Spirit will lift barrier among us to lead us to a new level of life; understand, communicate, and love. Mostly, speak the Gospel of salvation through Jesus Christ to everyone freely.

The Door is Open Wide:
By entering the wide open door
John 3:16-17

People think that Christian life is hard. It is true to live a good Christian life is not easy because we have to be a good model for other people. However, this concept misleads some people to think that the salvation is as hard to lift up the heavy rock. However, I want to say that the door for the salvation is widely open and God do not want to put any stumbling block to the door of salvation. There are four reasons for that. This perspective will lead us in to a new level of relationship with Christ. Don't sweat; I will make it easy for you.

I. We get salvation not by our Merit, but by Grace

In the prayer of the Pharisees, they had three thanks and those are, 'Lord, thank you that I was not born as women, not as tax collector, not as a pagan.' To them pagan means all other races and all other religious groups. This religious group was so exclusive. They pushed people out. On the other hand, there were sinners and tax collectors who dared not to look up heaven when they prayed. They just beat their beasts and said, "Lord have mercy on me". Whose prayer do you think God would want to accept? God accepted the prayer of those who felt that they were unworthy, weak, and miserable. Do you feel that you are not worthy to get salvation? Do not worry, the salvation is ready for you as it was ready for those who prayed with sinner' attitude. Christ opens the door widely for all of us. John 3: 16 says, "For God so loved the world that He gave His one and only begotten Son so that whoever believes in His name shall not perish, but have everlasting life." Christ makes double secure in the next word in verse 17 about the love of God. It says, "God did not sent His Son into the world to condemn, but that the world through Him might be saved" Therefore, God's grace make the door of salvation widely open as the door of the city of refuge was widely opened.

II. Salvation will be given to those who even have a little Faith

In Matthew 9: 20-26, we can see the woman who touched Christ's cloth with little faith like a mustard seed. She told herself, "If only I touch his cloak, I will be healed". Neither had she taken hold of Christ' whole body, nor put arms around. She just touched the edge of Jesus' cloth. She had not just the physical bleeding, but emotional bleeding. She felt that she would not be accepted from others. She even doubted that if she would be accepted by Christ because she had experienced so many hurts. So, she was hesitated to touch Christ although she had strong desire to touch Christ. However, Jesus healed her right there and looked for her and encouraged her faith saying, "Take heart and your faith healed you". It was amazing statement. Although you have a little faith or shy faith like this woman, trust that Jesus would take your little faith very positively. Even if it would be a small like a mustard seed, Jesus will accept and make it grow as a big tree.

Do you remember that Jesus accepted the thief on the cross? On his desperate moment, he did not claim for his salvation because he felt that he was not worthy to be saved. He just asked to Christ, 'Lord, remember me in your kingdom' The Lord answered the desperate prayer of the man who was waiting for the execution. Jesus said, 'You will be with me today in the paradise.'

III. God even will give salvation to those who are fearful and have doubts (Matthew 8:23-27)

When the disciples were afraid of the raged waves, Christ rebuked them, "Why are you fearful Oh! You of little faith" Although Jesus rebuked their doubts, He did not condemn them and accepted them as they were and calmed the storm. Jesus calmed the horrible situation and rescued them. He will accept you even if you are fearful and have doubts.

IV. God's salvation is even possible for the weak person

It seems like the theory of Darwin which says, 'survival is only for the fittest and the strongest' is working in our society .In every society, whether it is hidden or expressed there are food cycle. So, everybody try to be strong. It seems like there is no place for the weak person in this world, even in the church. But thank God that He loves the weak and shows more concern for them. Jesus had more concern for the sick and those who had a lower social status. Jesus loved children and gave respect to the women and sinners in His life time.

Isaiah chapter 11 says, "The wolf will live with the lamb, the leopard will lie down with the goat, the calf and the lion and the yearling together.... the infant will play near the hole of the cobra, ... there will be neither harm nor destroy..." (Isaiah 11: 6-9) Why the garden pictured by Isaiah in 11:6-9 is a paradise? Because it is the place where everybody can get along and live together. Even if you are not strong, you will be accepted just like others in there. Christ will welcome even the weak person. As it was described in Isaiah, the Lord's reign is the place where the wolf and the lambs dwell together and the young lion play with the calves.

Christ will never exclude anyone. He will accept all. He will open the door of salvation widely and remove all the hindrances to become our refuge. Do you feel that you are unworthy, shameful, guilty, and weak? Are you fearful?

Just trust God and His Son Jesus! He will accept you as you are. Just come straight to Him! God's love in Christ is for everyone. He will always widely open the gate of His refuge. With this belief and perspective, you will get new life.

The City of Refuge: Entering the refuge that God prepared
Numbers Chapter 35

There is sometimes tribulation in our lives. You may have to face the difficulties, accusations. If you do not have person to turn around and have no place to go, what do you do? Do not worry. Christ will welcome you and be your refuge. And the more good news is that the door is widely open to everyone. Christ is like a high priest who makes sure to get rid of all the hindrance in coming to the city of refuges. John 3:16 said, "Whoever believes in his name shall not perish, but have everlasting life". Remember, 'whoever' means that there would be no restriction and favoritism for the salvation because the door of salvation is opened for everyone. So, just run straight to Christ. Let us remember that king's high way is widely opened and it is safe and clear. It is easy enough to just run straight to the refuge. Although we have heavy burden in our minds with the thought about the furious avenger's blood and the thought about the wrath of God, just run fast to the refuge of God. Is the thought of 'am I going to be accepted, not punished!' stick to your mind? I want you to keep in mind what Jesus said, "I will give you rest. Take my yoke upon you and learn from me for I am gentle and humble in heart and you will find rest for your souls." (Matthew 11: 29-30) Give all your burdens to Christ. Just run straight to Christ, since the door is widely opened. Christ is your refuge and you will have rest in there.

Moses 5 books are called as Pentateuch. Those are Genesis, Exodus, Leviticus, Numbers, and Deuteronomy. Among those 5, the fourth book is named as 'Numbers'. In the Hebrew Old Testament; it is titled as 'In the Wilderness' because it is the record of the Israelites life in the wilderness. Think about this, more than 600,000 Israel people had wondered around 40 years together in the wilderness where there were little water and food. Imagine how many family and social problems would had happened in the wilderness. I am sure that there would be lots of social problems. They were all in the desert and not settled yet, still have lots of problems. So, this law came not only make them as Godly people but it came out of necessity for solving their society problems. God gave Moses the law and the detail regulations in the book of 'Numbers' (In the wilderness) as practical law that the Israelites should apply in their life in the wilderness. So, as a necessity, Moses set up lots of rules and regulation around the axiom of Ten-Commandment. Moses regulation seemed just strict and it was. However, through these Pentateuch, God also showed us fundamental truth of salvation, which was fully echoed in John 3:16 of the New Testament. In this book, there is an interesting law called, 'the city of refuge'. I never looked at the Old Testament as a reflection of God's grace until I read this story. When the children of Israel were settled in Cannon, God ordered them to set apart certain cities to be called as the Cities of refuges that those the man/women slayer might flee for security. He ordered to build 6 big cities and 42 small size cities to set-aside as cities of refuge. If one killed another, but had no intention for malice, he/she might flee at once to the city of refuge and if one could enter its gates before the avenger of blood captured him, he/she would be secure. The high priest had responsibility and the right to guarantee the protection of the refugees who flee to hide. Nobody could take them out from the territory of the priest. (Numbers 35:6, 11) It was Mosaic Law and civil law as well in those days. Since the 'City of Refuge' should be one element of their promised land which was their dreamland, the sacred place of the city of refuge is essential to make a dreamland. Catholic learned well from that. It amazed me that one part of the Mosaic Law was the rule of setting 'city of refuge', that which foreshadowed the graceful salvation of Christ. This law was made out of the necessity for the society because if they allowed avenging with outraged anger, there would be more blood and cruelty. Most of all, this law shows that, "There is a place for God's mercy even in the Mosaic law." The law of 'the city of refuge' is the shadow of God's grace that would come through Jesus Christ.

Let me share what I have learned from Rev Spurgeon's book about the city of refugee. Once a year or more often the magistrates of the district were accustomed to survey the high roads, which led to these cities. They carefully gathered up all the stones and took the greatest possible precaution that there should be no stumbling blocks in the way so that there would be no cause for the poor fugitive to fall. High priests had to make sure that it would be carried on. And moreover, along the road, there were hand-posts with the word, 'refuge' written very clearly so that when the fugitive came to a cross-road, he might not need to question for a single moment to think, "Which way is the escape?" He needed to head on to the clearly marked 'City of Refuge'. Once he got in there, he was secured completely. You may have read many times that the Psalmist songs, "The Lord is my refuge. The Lord is my rock, my fortress and my strength". If you relate this Psalm with the 'City of Refuge' in Mosaic Law, it would give you better understanding of the meaning of salvation.

Perspective that leads to new life: How are we able to get new life?

Psalms 1:1-3 says, "Blessed is the man who delights meditating the word of God day and night. He is like a tree planted by streams of water, which yields its fruit in season." The word of God gives us a new perspective of life and it leads us to have a great new life; hopeless person will change to be a hopeful person, negative person will change to a positive thinker, and sick person will be changed to a healthy person. As a result, they will have a fruitful life like a tree planted by streams of water.

God's compassion
Isaiah 49:14-21

In olden days, Israelites once were under the captivity of the Babylonian Empire for about 430 years. After the Israelites lost the war, they became slaves to the Babylonians. It was a sorrowful, long exile. Listen to one of the songs they sang, "I was bereaved and barren. I was exiled and rejected. Who brought these up? I was left all alone." (Isaiah 49:21)

When our loved ones leave us, we feel rejected. More painful than the pain of disease is the feeling of rejection and the thought that the Lord has forgotten me. The Israelites felt that God abandoned them. So, Zion (Mount Zion was the central focus the Israelites) said in Isaiah 49:14, "The Lord has forsaken me, the Lord has forgotten me." Today's scripture is the answer to that mourning. Isaiah 49:15 said: "Can a Mother forget the baby at her breast and have no compassion on the child she has borne?" Think about your Mother's love when it is hard to have faith in God's love and God's care for you. Think about the words, "Can a Mother forget the baby at her breast? Can a Mother who has borne her child have no compassion for the baby?"

The Garden of Eden that God had created should be a perfectly happy land, where there were no sorrows or pains. It was a Paradise. However, even in this perfectly happy and painless land, there was a minor pain. Do you know what only one pain was in the pain free garden? It was the pain of childbirth. When God had punished Eve after the fall, God said, "I will greatly increase your pains in childbearing; with pain you will give birth to children." Listen carefully to the words, "increase your pain." It means that God had already designed to have pain in childbirth even in Paradise, although it was far less discomfort than what women experience now in delivering their babies. I give a thought about this scripture for a while. I found that there was a reason why God made the principle of painful childbirth. It was because God wanted us to learn the importance of life. From the very moment of the

Garden of Eden, God put mothers in a special place. God imbedded life into women. And it is the mother who passes the inheritance of faith to their child.

Moses had two mothers; one was Pariah's daughter, a princess who saved him when his family was forced to throw their beautiful baby-boy into the Nile River. He also had his own physical birth Mother who became his nurse. Since he was adopted as the son of the princess of Egypt, he grew up as a prince and enjoyed all the privileges and education of a prince. However, in all of Egypt's kingly court there was none who could pass down the faith of the Lord, Yahweh. With God's providence, Moses' birth mother raised him in her role as his nurse. She taught him and raised him as a believer of God, the God of Yahweh.

In the life of our Lord, Christ Jesus, Christ' mother Mary held a special place in His Heart. On the cross, Jesus told His disciple, "Woman, this is your son." Jesus said this, because Jesus wanted to take care of His Mother who would suffer of losing her Son by connecting her with John as compensation and the way of comfort. Mary, as the Mother of Jesus, deserved this because she took care of Jesus with compassion, many efforts of love, and sacrifices.

As a conclusion, let me refer back to today's scripture, which reminds us of the compassion and faithful love of God who would never forsake us. "Can a mother forget the baby at her breast?" Do you feel abandoned? Remember that God is like a Mother who could never forget the baby she raised. God has compassionate heart like a Mother who gives compassion to her baby. Never will He forsake you in any circumstance. I had read an article where all people on an airplane had died in an airplane-crash when it was landing except one baby, because her Mother embraced her. In the city of Pompae, during the volcano a Mother embraced and protected her baby and died for the baby. The statue of the mother holding her baby still remained in an ancient city. In like manner, God, the Son Jesus died on the cross to save us from eternal damnation. This God will never forsake you. Trust and have faith in God's love. Also learn to appreciate the love of your mother whose love resembles God's love. Our perspective about your mother should be healthy, and it will lead us to a new life. Deepen our understanding of God's love so that we would have full abundant life.

God's sacrificial love
John 3:16

Mother Teresa, who was awarded the Nobel peace prize in 1980 said, "True love hurts ". She continued, "It hurts God when He gave His only begotten Son to the world. It hurt Jesus when He died on the cross; it hurt His Mother, Mary to see her precious Son suffering on the cross."

If we truly believe and understand the love of God that was shown on the cross, we will understand that Jesus hurt Himself on the cross to give us salvation and the real joy of life. When God allowed Governor Pilate and the Pharisees and the people to crucify Jesus on the cross, God actually was being crucified Himself. When Jesus was on the cross and suffering, the pain was unbearable that Jesus cried, "Eloi Eloi Lama Sabakdani, which means, My God, My God why have you forsaken me?" The physical pain was unbearable. The most painful thing for Jesus Christ was His separation from God and a feeling of abandonment. There are some people who ask me, "You said, God and Jesus is one. How come Jesus cried to God and God abandoned Him? Aren't there two persons here?" It is not easy to answer to that particular question. However, I can say that when Jesus suffered, God was hurt just like Jesus because God truly loved Jesus and truly loved us.

It may be easy just to say that 'I love you'. However, practicing true love is difficult because it should be accompanied by sacrifice, commitment and effort toward the beloved and for the beloved. When Nicodemos spent all night and could not sleep because of the agony of life, Jesus Christ counseled him and said, "I would die and be hurt in your place to save you from the agony of life and to give you peace by saying, 'As Moses lifted up the serpent in the wilderness, even so the Son of man be lifted up that whoever believes in Him should not perish, but have eternal life'." Jesus was not just saying 'I love you'. Jesus died for Nicodemus and hurt Himself on the cross for us as well. He got hurt to save us. Jesus proved His love for us by hurting himself.

Apostle Paul said, "You see, at just the right time, when we were still powerless, Christ died for the ungodly. Very rarely will anyone die for a righteous man, but for a good man someone might dare to die. God demonstrates his true love for us. While we were still sinners, Christ died for us. "(Romans 5:6-8) In the King James Version, the word, 'demonstrates' was translated as 'proved'. God proved His love by putting Himself in our hurting place. Jesus Christ proved His love toward us by His death. I pray that we would understand how much God loved us so that we would have a new life with the new perspective of hurting love.

God's holy words transform your life
Acts 12: 1-24

We are weak, but God is strong. In the midst of the world turmoil and persecution, the word of God has life in itself and possesses a dynamic power, which multiplies and encourages His children. The Word of God makes people learn and accept Christ and helps them to know the way of getting new life. The Word of God gives people hope.

When Jesus Christ appeared to His disciples after His resurrection, He predicted that Peter would have a hard life, saying that "I tell you the truth, when you were younger you dressed yourself and went where you wanted; but when you are old you will stretch out your hands, and someone else will dress you and lead you where you do not want to go." Jesus said this to indicate the kind of death by which Peter would glorify God. (John 21:18-19) On another occasion, when Jesus first sent His disciples on their mission, He expressed concern for His disciples, "I am sending you out like sheep among wolves. Therefore be as shrewd as snakes and as innocent as doves." (Matthew 10: 16)

As Christ predicted, His disciples were like sheep among wolves. They were weak and had no wit to protect them. When I read the story in Acts 12, I felt like as if I were watching lions snatching prey; that is weak, unprotected, and defenseless as sheep. Think about sheep among wolves! How desperate they are! How much are they exposed to the risk of their lives without any protection! You have heard the word, 'scapegoat'. In the Mosaic Law, Moses made a law of redemption wherein he placed all the sins of the people to a goat. The goat was executed outside of the city and sacrificed just as a victim, no fault of his own. Now, we use the word scapegoat as the one who has to shoulder the blame due to another. King Nero used the Christians as his scapegoat. People were hostile to Nero because he burned the city of Rome due to his absurd ways and insanity. Their anger and outrage pressured and it was about to explode like the volcano. Nero, like a tricky wolf, directed the outrage and anger of the foolish crowds onto the innocent Christians. It was same technique used by King Herod in today's scripture. Herod used the disciples as a scapegoat.

The Herod in today's Scripture was the grandson of Herod the Great, who ruled at the time of Jesus' birth. Herod-the Great, had killed his own son, so Herod's grandson, known as Herod Agrippa I, was raised in Rome. He learned the Roman strategies of rising to the power. He made lots of political connections there, especially he made, Caligula, as his close friend. Later on, Caligula became the Emperor of Rome. With his help Herod Agrippa had all the territories of Judea and Samaria under his control and made himself as a king. He became a king with the backup of Rome. However, he realized that he also needed to get the support of the people to continue his political life. He found that the Jews hated the Christians. So he began to harass the leaders of the Christian Church in Jerusalem. He arrested some who belonged to the Church and started to persecute them. Soon after, he caught James, the brother of John, and put him death by the sword. He found that the Jews were so pleased about that tragedy that he proceeded to seize Peter also.

As the leader of a nation, Herod Agrippa should have tried to be a good model and to protect his people. Unfortunately, he was kind of one of those ancient wicked kings who just wanted to hold onto his power. Because of his cruelty and persecution, the Christianity from the outset was in danger. It seemed that the Church had no place to stand in the world. The apostles and the Christians were like defenseless sheep among wolves. They were beheaded, persecuted, and misunderstood. However, as we can read in today's scripture, God- the almighty living Lord was on their side.

God had helped Peter to escape from the prison miraculously. (Verses 6-11) While Peter remained in prison, he was guarded by four sets of four guards each day. Peter was chained to two soldiers by day and by night. It was impossible to escape. But while Peter was asleep, an angel appeared unexpectedly in the cell and a supernatural light flooded the prison. The angel urged Peter to get up quickly, "Put on your clothes and sandals, wrap your cloth around you and follow me." The angels brought Peter out of the jail, walking past the sleeping guards without anyone stopping them. The last gate, an iron gate, opened of its own accord and they went out into the street. There the angel left Peter, and then Peter now came fully awake and realized that the Lord had sent His angel to deliver him.

King Herod, who persecuted the Christians and assumed the role of a god, receiving temporal glory from the people, was eaten by worms and died miserably. But the word of God continued to increase and the Gospel was spread. "The word of God continued to increase and spread." In the King James Bible, it translates, "But the word of God grew and multiplied." This statement was repeated 6 times throughout the whole book of Acts as summary of the stories of the act of the Holy Spirit. (Acts 6:7, 9:31, 16:5, 19:20, 28:31) The Acts concluded its story in chapter19:20, "In this way the word of the Lord spread widely and grew in power." The last verse of Acts wrote, "Boldly and without hindrance he preached the kingdom of God and taught about the Lord Jesus Christ." These words were not the end story of Acts, but it was continuing repeating story of the acts of the Christians as the Holy Spirit continues to work. This Story never ends. It continues to the present moment.

Why is it so important that the word of God spreads and grow in power? It is because the word of God is the focus agent of God's redemptive work. And the word of God, which is centered in the Gospel of Christ, is the power of God for the salvation of everyone who believes. For in the Gospel of Christ righteousness from God is revealed. In the gospel of Christ, there are the wisdom and the power to be saved, redeemed, sanctified and glorified. The word of God is the power for the reconciliation of all people and it gives hope.

We are weak and defenseless like sheep. But remember that the living God is our deliverer and protector and our banner of victory. Most of all, He will help us spread the word of God. Worry, fear, and anxiety penetrate into our hearts and put us in chains when we focus solely on our weakness. But remember that nothing can bind us and even an iron gate cannot hold us in prison forever, because the living God is with us. As Paul said, "In all these things we are more than conquerors through Him who loved us. If God, the almighty living God is with us, who can be against us? I am convinced that nothing can separate us from the love of God that is in Christ Jesus our Lord. " (Romans 8:37-39) Jesus said, "Are not two sparrows sold for a penny yet not one of them will fall to the ground apart from the will of your Father. And even the hairs of your head are all numbered. So do not be afraid; you are worth more than many sparrows." (Matthew 10: 29-31)

Do you know the number of strands of hair on your head? We have no way to count those. But God knows! He knows your situation, every single problem and concern. And nothing in the world that has life, even the lowly sparrow, who's only worth is a penny, cannot lose its life without our Lord's will, because our Lord is the sovereign of the world and of the universe. And more importantly is the knowledge that He values us highly. In fact, Christ considers one life more valuable than the whole universe. So, do not be afraid. Look to the future and nothing will harm you.

GOD SHOWS HIS LOVE IN THREE WAYS:
1ˢᵗ John 4:7-12

Today, we live in a society where the technology is so highly developed that people even attempt to reach to Mars. I am sure that you remember the excitement when astrologists in Pasadena successfully sent a computer-generated robot to Mars. Highly developed technology helps us to achieve higher goals. It gives us the advantage of convenience and more luxuries for our lives. However, the society that we are now living in is so competitive that people are suffering from loneliness. The most serious problem that we would face in this 21 century is the problem of loneliness. One day a couple came to my office to unburden them. We dialogued well together. They wanted to be reassigned to Germany. Wife was a German lady and she wanted to be with her mother in Germany. To help them with the details, I asked the wife about her mother's profile. The woman brought the medical profile of her mother to my office. A German Dr. wrote that the disease of the mother was 'LONELINESS'. The physician actually listed loneliness as a disease: 'Die Einsamkeit'. The woman's mother had nobody around her after the death of her husband. She, indeed, suffered from loneliness. All she needed was to have her daughter or some close member of the family stay and live with her. I still do not have the answer to whether loneliness is a disease or a problem. However, I do know that loneliness is a major issue for modern people. How do we take care of this issue? To overcome loneliness, we have to remember the love of God because knowing the love of God is the surest way to heal loneliness. Love, in fact, is the essential virtue of Christianity. In the first letter of John, the Apostle John said, "God is love, whoever lives in love lives in God and God in him." (1st John 4:16) In the letter addressed to the saints of the Corinthians the Apostle, Paul, revealed that the highest value in the life of a Christian is love. He said: "And now I will show you the most excellent way. If I speak in the tongues of men and of angels, but I have not love, I am only a resounding gong or a clanging cymbal. If I have the gift of prophesy and can fathom all mysteries and all knowledge, and if I have a faith that can move mountains but have not love, I am nothing. If I give all possessions to the poor and surrender my body to the flames, but have not love, I gain nothing." (1st Corinthian 13:1-3) The deepest quality of God is not His Power, but His Love for us.

Now, how does God show His love? In many ways, of course, but I just want to focus on three.

First, God sacrificed His Only Son, Jesus Christ for our salvation. I cannot over-emphasize the love of God shown to us at the Cross of Jesus. By His nature, Jesus is God. Hebrews 1:1-5 said that Jesus, God's Son is the One appointed as the heir of all things, and through who also God created the world. He reflects the glory of God and bears the very stamp of His nature, upholding the universe by his word of power. The Son, therefore, is the radiance of God's glory and the exact representation of His being. However, Jesus came down to us as a human being. The Creator who created stars and the universe shrink into nothing, and came down to our level to live with us. Why? What is the purpose for His coming down to us? It is primarily for our salvation, then, to befriend us and finally to restore relationships for you and me with God.

Jesus regards us as His friend, for He has said in John 15:13-15 "Greater love has no one than this that he lay down his life for his friends. You are my friends, if you do what I command. I no longer call you servants, because a servant does not know his Master's business. Instead, I called you friends, for I have made known to you everything that I learned from my Father." The cross of Jesus Christ is not a superficial event. The cross is the expression of the intimate love of God for us. Jesus came down as our friend and He died for his friends. Knowing this friendly sacrifice is the best remedy for healing the problem of loneliness. Knowing God's love, knowing this intimate relationship of being a friend of God should change the heart of any lonely person.

To illustrate how deep the friendship between God and us, I refer to the beautiful story in the Old Testament where David and Jonathan are united. The story took place just after David had defeated Goliath. You can find this story in 1st Samuel 18:1-2. It reads, "When he had finished speaking to Saul, the soul of Jonathan was knit to the soul of David, and Jonathan loved him as his own soul. And Saul took him that day, and would not let him return to his father's house." Jonathan made a covenant with David, one of close friendship. As proof of his good intentions, Jonathan took off his robe, tunic, belt as well as his sword. Normally, this would have been a difficult move for Jonathan, since David was his political opponent. Jonathan also thought that he, as a prince, should be the successor of the King. However, Jonathan had even saved David's life on many occasions. By giving his tunic as well as his sword, Jonathan foreshadowed the intense love of Jesus Christ for us. Later, when Jonathan died in a war, David made a song for him: 'How the mighty have fallen in battle. Jonathan lies slain on your heights. I grieve for you, my brother, Jonathan. You were dear to me. Your love for me was more wonderful than that of woman.'

Do you have a friend like Jonathan who really cares about you? The reason people experience burnout is not because of the workload but because of a lack of a concerned and friendly ear, where they can talk about their burdens when they are depressed. If you have found one friend with whom you can share your burdens, your problems, and your joys, you have succeeded in your life.

It is important to have a friendship like David and Jonathan. Most of all, it is important to find Jesus Christ, your friend who died for you.

Second, God showed His Love by waiting for us patiently. A young teenager, who was still immature but curious about the world unknown to him, asked his father one day, "Give me all of my inheritance, now." With all the money the father gave to him, he left and ran out of his father's house. He lived frivolously, wasted all his money until a famine came. Then this teenager began to starve, begging for food. So desperate was he that he even wanted to eat the scraps that the pigs would eat, but no one offered him the opportunity. Oh, how he wanted to go back home! But he felt he could not because of what he had done to his father. Finally he decided to return home. As he returned to his home, he thought that his father would never accept him. He just wanted to fill up with his stomach and hired as a servant. But while he was still a long way off, his father saw him even though the young man was barely distinguishable, wearing tattered clothes and had a grimy face. The father still recognized him and filled with compassion for him. The father ran to his son and he threw his arms around and kissed the son.

How the father was able to recognize his son even though the son was disheveled and frayed? It was because the father kept waiting and waiting for his son to come back. It was easy for the father to recognize his son with his heart.

God constantly waits for us, even at times when we go against His Will. Even at the time when we stray far away from God, He does not abandon us. Although He remains silent, He waits for us to come back because he loves us with the deepest affection. I would like to cite Romans 10:21: "All day I have held my hands to a disobedient and obstinate people." God opens up His Arms wide, waiting for you to come back!

The third way that God showed his love is in his discipline. Hebrews 12: 5-7 is an encouraging message in a very discouraging situation. In our society, we are beginning to lose this third concept of God's love because society has become so much more permissive to sin. You can see that things are just not right. However, God's love is not the love that spoils His children. Nevertheless, when difficulties occur, we must approach the situation as a measure of God's love. We must understand it happens because of God's disciplining love. That is exactly what the book of Hebrews said, "And have you forgotten the exhortation which addresses you as sons? My sons, do not regard lightly the discipline of the Lord, nor lose courage when you are punished by Him, for the Lord disciplines him whom he loves." (Hebrews12: 5-6)

When God disciplines you, do not be afraid because God will make everything that befalls ultimately benefit you for your life in the long term.

God loves us and shows us his love in many ways, especially by i) sacrificing His Son for our salvation, ii) waiting patiently for our genuine response to His love, iii) and sometimes disciplining. Therefore, let us not be discouraged in any circumstances and have confidence on God's unconditional love. Look at God, who really loves us, it will lead us to the new life. Amen.

REDEEMED LIFE OF RUTH
Ruth 4: 1-18

Up in the front; let me tell what the story of Ruth tells us today. This story foreshadows how Jesus Christ could become our Redeemer. As you know, Ruth has a special position in the genealogy of Christ. Although she was a Moabite woman, she became the grandmother of King David and ancestor of our Lord, Jesus Christ. Matthew's Gospel records it specifically. It is in the Gospel of Matthew 1:5-6. The beautiful story of the redemption of Ruth preceded the story of the birth of Jesus Christ, our Redeemer. The great prophet during the period of the Babylonian Captivity, the Dark age of Israel, Isaiah prophesied: "The Redeemer will come out from the Family of Boaz whose son is Jesse. There shall come forth a shoot from the stump of Jesse, and a branch shall grow out of his roots. And the Spirit of the Lord shall rest upon Him, the Spirit of wisdom and understanding." (Isaiah 11:1-2) Boaz is a fore-shadow of Christ. To free us from the bondage of sin and death, Christ fully paid the price and He saved us with His blood.

There are many stories in the Bible, especially in the Old Testament. So, Old Testament is a story book. In this book, some stories end sadly, some stories end with joy. What kind of story do you like? Do you like stories with sad endings or ones with happy endings? Many secular stories end with bitterness, but the stories of God unfold differently. It may start with mourning and sorrow but end with happiness and victory. The story of Ruth is the greatest example of this kind of story.

I want to introduce a happy ending story of Ruth. This book starts with a famine and three funerals in one family, but it ends with the wedding of Boaz with Ruth and the birth of the forefather of Jesus Christ. Boaz and Ruth, with her mother in law and her grand son, Obed, made a sweet home in Bethlehem.

Let's first look at the background story. This story started with a tragedy that happened in the little town of Bethlehem, which is the hometown of Jesus Christ. Bethlehem means the 'house of bread'. But the bread ran out at the house of bread. A famine struck this little town of Judea. So, Naomi' husband and their two sons left Bethlehem with all of their families and moved to Moab, which was the foreign land for them and their sons.

While they were living there for ten years, their sons married Moabite women. There, Naomi's husband died and after few years, her two sons died. The sons did not leave any children. So, only three widows were left. The mother and the two daughters-in-law all became widows. It was a widow fellowship. Can you imagine how lonesome Naomi was and how sorrowful she was?

Her name, Naomi, meant 'pleasant and delightful'. When her parents named her Naomi, they wanted her to have a happy and delightful life. However, because of the famine and the death of her husband and sons, her life became miserable and bitter. She was greeted by the hometown folk, "How are you, Naomi-the delightful lady?" She told them, "Do not call me Naomi, please, call me Mara, for the Almighty has dealt very bitterly with me."

After the Israelites exiled from Egypt and wandered around the wilderness of Sinai, they encountered a serious water problem. Many of them died because they drank polluted water. At that time they called that place 'Mara', which means bitterness. Naomi's life now became bitter like the polluted water in the desert. So, she wanted her name changed to Mara. Evil brought tragedy to all three women. Naomi and two daughters-in-law in particular, named Ruth, became bitter.

However, the conclusion of this story ended with great joy, happiness, and triumph. Let us look at how the bitterness became a story with a happy ending. These women might have thought that their lives would end with no hope for tomorrow. They had no idea where to go. Furthermore, they could never imagine that they would become the vessel of the birth of the Messiah. Their only concern was how to survive. However, God had constantly worked in their lives. God had a providential plan for them. God's grace worked in their lives through a man named Boaz, who became a kinsman-redeemer of Ruth. The first chapter of this story highlights famine and death. If a famine happened to us, we might think of the crisis as a dead end. But in this beautiful story the sad beginning chapter is only temporary and moves toward the unfolding of a happy story because God's Hand involved in their lives.

In ancient Hebrew family law, if one's brother died and left a widow without son, a brother or next of kinsman of the deceased man was required to marry the widow. And a son be born to such a marriage should be considered as the child of the deceased. This is called a levitate marriage and its origin was the law of redemption. This law originated from Leviticus 25:23-34, which is the law for the redemption of the land and the people from slavery. The purpose of these laws was to preserve the family name and to protect the families' property for those who unfortunately lost their land and family origin.

The redeemer in Hebrew is called the goel, and it means a family member who redeems the property of his next of kin when such property has been sold because of debt. Leviticus 25:25 says, "If your brother becomes poor and sells part of his property, then his next of kin shall come and redeem what his brother has sold." This same principle is applied to the redemption of a person from slavery. Leviticus 25: 47-49 says, "If a stranger or sojourner with you becomes rich, and your brother beside him becomes poor and sells himself to the stranger, one of his brother may redeem him, or his uncle, his cousin may redeem him."

"To redeem" means "to set free by paying a certain price." This law was extended as the law of levirate ("levir" means "a husband's brother") marriage, which was explained in Deuteronomy 25:5-10. Since we are not familiar with their law, let us look at Scripture of Deuteronomy 25: 5, 6. It says, "If brothers are living together and one of them dies without a son, his widow must not marry outside the family. Her husband's brother shall take her and marry her. This marriage would fulfill the duty of a brother to her. The first son she bears shall carry on the name of the dead brother so that his name will not be blotted out from Israel." It is a requirement, a duty as a brother, not a choice on those days. If this brother does not want to obey the law, what will happen? His life will be shameful because he does not want to build up his brother's family line. I do not think we have to apply this law in today's Christian life nor does God require us to do so. However, this law gives us a profound principle of life - the love of redeeming others: give our possessions and our lives to set our brothers and sisters free!

Now, let us see how Boaz could become the redeemer of Ruth.

First of all, Boaz was compassionate to Ruth's family and loved Ruth with 'Agape love.' Because of his love toward Ruth, he was very generous to Ruth. He tried to supply what their family needed. Because of his love, Boaz did his best to find a redeemer for her. Eventually, he himself became her kinsman-redeemer.

Ruth was a foreigner, a Moabite and a poor lady. The only thing she had was a good reputation as a sincere and loving person. She had inner beauty and was loyal to her mother-in-law. Outwardly, she had nothing. Ruth had definitely no material blessings. Since she was one of the Moabites, the Jews would not want to associate with her. In fact, she was despised just because she was a tribe of Moabites. Also, Ruth was once married and had only a small parcel of land that was passed out of the family ownership. So, no person wanted to be a redeemer of Ruth. However, Boaz stepped forward and said, "Pass it unto me. I will take Ruth as my wife." He said to the surrounding people who witnessed. "Today you witnessed that I bought from Naomi all the property of Elimelichm Killon and Mahlon to maintain the name of the dead with his property." (9-10)

Second, Boaz was an able man. Even if someone had a generous heart and was willing to be a redeemer, if he was not able to pay the redemption price, he still could not be the redeemer. Fortunately, Boaz was rich and could pay the price to set Ruth free. Our Lord Jesus

Christ could pay our debts because He was from God and has all-power of God.

Third, Boaz was willing to pay the price to be Ruth's *goel* (kinsmen-redeemer). He did not devalue the importance of marriage by making it as a bargain. The first line kinsman at first wanted to be a *goel*, but then he backed away because he just wanted to bargain for the land ownership. The first kinsman did not want to jeopardize his estate. But Boaz willingly paid the price for Ruth and the land. Boaz married her without any condition. Marriage described as a redeeming feature. Marriage relationship should come out from pure love, not as a bargain. There is also a strong bond in the relationship among the members of family and it will accompany responsibility. That make a security in this marriage and it will create a covenant society. Covenant Society here means to keep one's word. Boaz' relationship is formed by the model in the Jewish religion wherein God always keeps His word. Boaz will keep his word always.

God shows concern for common people like us. In old days, we were out-caster, broke, and lost. But, now Christ became our redeemer with His compassionate heart and Agape love. He paid all our debts and saved us. His redeeming action changed our status. God elevated us so that they may be dignified and respected by the people. Now, we can live a life of freemen/freewomen and dignified life.

CHAPTER 5

PRACTICE OF NEW LIFE

Jesus talked about the new life in the parable of the 'Old wineskins and the New wine". He said, "No one tears a patch from a new garment and sews it on an old one. If he does, he will have torn the new ferment, and the patch from the new will not match the old. And no one pours new wine into the old wineskins. If he does, the new wine will burst the skins, the wine will run out and the wineskins will be ruined. No, new wine must be poured into new wineskins. And no one after drinking old wine wants the new, for he says, 'The old is better.' " (Luke 5: 36-39)

People are uncomfortable to change their life style although they want new things and new life. However, as Jesus said, if they do not want to pour new wine into the new wineskins, it will burst out. We should pour new wine into the new wineskins.

After we have a new life, we should keep up living a new life. We should walk a new life, not just talk a new life. Then, we will really experience and enjoy the new life. In this chapter, I want to talk about what is the practice of new Christian life, which is a new wineskin.

1. Live a life of whose spirit is poor: Blessedness of the poor in spirit
2. Live a life of thanksgiving: Learn to appreciate
3. Forgive as the Father Forgave you

4. Imitate Christ' humility
5. Love your neighbor
6. Obey your parents
7. Focus on the future goal
8. Commit thy way to the Lord
9. Live a life with discerning heart
10. Live by the Spirit, not by might
11. Look up to God, Who Disciplines and Refines You like Gold in Times of Suffering
12. Live as a victor when life seems unfair
13. Live as a victor when life seems tough

Live a life of the blessing of those who are poor in spirit:
The Blessedness of those who are poor in spirit
Matthew 5: 1-3

Throughout the human history and all over the world, human desires the happiness of life. People are hunger for the happiness and run after the happiness. People struggles for the happiness, even die for the happiness. By the way, what is happiness, how we get it and when are we happy? With this topic in our mind, I would like talk, "who are really blessed".

To get real happiness, we need the good map to reach to happiness. Dag Hammarskjold, the secretary general of the United Nations, died in an air crash on September 18, 1961 in Zambia, Central Africa. The general Dag Hammarkjold' plane pilot started to fly to the NADOLA, Zambia, which was their destination. But the pilot carried the wrong map. Instead of the map of NADOLA, the pilot carried the map of NADOLO.

The pilot couldn't find out their destination until he had crashed his plane in open field at night. Thinking that he was at Nadola, where there were thousand more feet of landing strip than Nadolo, he landed and crashed. He had followed the wrong map. The only difference of the local names was an "A" and "O" and it made the difference between life and death. If we follow the wrong map of happiness, we can't reach on real God's blessing and happiness of life. Christ's sermon on the 8 Beatitudes gives right map for the happiness.

Let me first tell you this; Jesus came into the world to bless us. Now, this is the story. When Jesus went up to the mountain and sat down, his disciples came to him. And Jesus taught them the secret ways to get the blessing as He started his word, "Blessed are those!" Christ begins his sermon with blessing because he came into the world to bless us. When he blesses, he blesses with the authority as the one who commands and makes blessing. There is strong power in our words. As in the book of James, our tongue is smallest part of the body, but the most powerful part among our body. It can be used either as destructive or constructive depending on how you use it. With our tongue, we can pronounce blessing and cursing. Primitive religion emphasizes the power of the curse. Through magic and incantations, the Shaman or witch thought that they could bring the curse to the people. The story in Numbers chapter 23, 24 tells us regarding the primitive religion and cursing. The king of Moab gave lots of money to hire Ballam, depraved priest, to curse Israel. This is the story of donkey shows up as the animal, who rebukes his owner. Even Jesus talked about the power of tongue, which can be used as very destructive instrument. Jesus said, "Anyone who says, you fool will be in danger of the fire of hell". Telling others as, "Fool" was regarded as murder to Christ because it was a cursing. After the fall, human races share the curse of Satan and have tried to get rid of the curse. By receiving the blessings of God, human races want to return to the formal blessed state. The good news that Bible brings to us is that God wanted to bless all humankind and chose Abraham with the plan to bless all nations. As God called Abraham he said, "You will be the source of blessing and all humankind will be blessed by you".

Blessing others with our mind and word, and actions is very important. A famous football player, who became a prison minister later in his life, said that 99.9 % of the prisoner didn't get their parents' blessing and they got, instead, cursing from their parents. He says, "Father, mother, leaders, commanders, bless your kids, your subordinates from bottom of your hearts. Then, they will never go wrong way. They will be your crown, prosperity and happiness". In the Jewish society, father's blessing is very important. It may be more important than the inheritance. That is why Bible described the long story of Jacob and Essau and their struggles to get the blessing of their father, Isaac. To us, it seemed not as big issue, because it was only a few words, neither stocks nor material inheritances. However, Jacob spent all his life to get the blessing of his father, just to hear from his father's saying, "May God gives you of heaven's dew and of the earth's richness"

In the story of movie, 'Play violin on the roof', which is the Jewish traditional story, one of his daughters was going to marry with a boy that the father didn't want because he was a poor musician. The daughter was about to leave her father without blessings. Her sister urgently asked the father for his blessing to her sister, "Father, let her go with your blessing". The father felt compassion to the daughter and said, "God bless you". It was a short word. But it was from his heart. His daughter joined to the violinist happily. Do we get blessing from our fathers, teachers and pastors? Do we bless our kids, subordinates? Kids, subordinates! Don't say that all I need from my parents or boss is practical help; good pay or get something else that I want. Wait and work with the patience to get their blessing and their recognition that comes from their hearts. Parents, leaders! Remember your blessing to your kids stay forever in their life. It will be more than other inheritances and more precious than thousand pounds of gold.

Unfortunately, there are parents and leaders and even pastors do not know the importance of blessing for their children and flocks. However, the good news is that Jesus Christ now pronounces the blessing with the authority of heaven, "Blessed are you"

Then, what is the blessing? "Blessed" in modern word is exactly same with the word, "Happiness". Everyone have different opinion about the happiness. Good relationship with the spouse, prosperity, healthy, children going well, good income, and promotion could bring us happiness. Of course, those are God's blessing as well. However, the measurement of Christ blessing is different than ours. Jesus, on the Sermon on the Mount laid the principles of blessing as he laid the 8 principles of blessing; Poor in spirit, Mourn, Meekness, Merciful heart, Purity of heart, Hunger and thirst for the righteousness, Peace-maker, Persecuted for the righteousness. All of those are inner strength and all blessings Jesus talked are related with our character. So, it is more important "Who we are" than "What do we possess". Our blessedness cannot be materialized and it cannot be measured by our measurements.

The first beatitude is "Blessed are those who are poor in spirit, for theirs is the kingdom of God" The general opinion is; "Blessed are those who are rich and possesses honorable position in the world". Paradoxically, Jesus said, "Blessed are those who are poor in spirit" This word seems very paradoxical. But there is truth in His word.

What is meaning of "Poor in spirit"? Before I go into detail, let me give my conclusion, 'Poor in spirit' means 'humble spirit'. To make it clear, let me first tell you what 'poor in spirit' does not mean. It does not mean the economic poverty. The Bible does not teach 'poverty' as a desirable thing. Becoming poor, is no credit or advantage to get into His kingdom because poverty does not guarantee spirituality. Poverty can lead us to be humble. Difficult situation can be God's discipline to mold us as humble person. However, it does not mean that you have to be poor to become spiritual. I have to tell you this because there are some confusion about material and Christianity. There are many poor people who rely upon material things exactly as many as the riches do.

Poor in spirit does not mean self-depreciation; to look down on one's self or to feel unworthy compared to other. Poor in spirit does not mean cowardliness, weak, discouraged, wormlike, low self-esteem. Contrary, Jesus Christ encouraged us to have confidence about ourselves and feel good about our images, instead of possessing inferior self-image. Christ met Simon, whose name meant as sand. His first word for Simon was, "You will be called, 'Peter', which means stable and huge rock. When Christ saw the persecutor Saul, he saw great missionary. When Christ saw a despised and lonely Samaritan woman who came to Jacob's well, he saw one soul who was seeking for spiritual water and the truth.

Then, what is the meaning of poor in spirit? Lloyd Jones who served as a minister of the Westminster Chapel at London said, "Poor in spirit means a complete absence of pride, a complete absence of self-assurance, realizing that we are nothing in the presence of God. It means humble spirit."

I would like to give two life examples of who are 'poor in spirit'.

First example is Christ who became a man and took upon him the likeness of sinful flesh. Though he was equal with God, he emptied himself and totally depended upon God, the Father, and said, "I can do nothing without God". (John 14) In his prayer life, he humbly kneeled down before Him, he completely relied upon God, the Father, with his spirit of poverty. This Jesus invites us for his peace and humbleness saying, "Come to me, all you are weary and burdened, and I will give you rest. Take my yoke upon you and learn from me, for I am gentle and humble in heart, and you will find rest for your souls. For my yoke is easy and my burden is light." (Matthew 11:9)

Second example is Paul. He possessed many conditions that he could be arrogant and boast of himself. But after he had met the Lord on the road to Damascus, he became 'poor in spirit'. Before he met Christ, he felt no need for help from anybody. He felt completely self-sufficient. However, after the conversion, he became poor in spirit. He found himself as helpless sinner. He confessed later, "Without God's help, I can't do anything. But I can do everything through him who gives me strength" (Philippians 4:20)

There is no one who is not poor in spirit in the kingdom of God. Blessed are those who are poor in spirit! In modern language, it can be said, "Happy are those who have emptied their vain pride and humbly accept the love and the power of God because God's peace and love will remain in their hearts."

BOOK 5: NEW LIFE

Live a life of Thanksgiving: Learn to Appreciate
Luke 17: 11-19

Psalm 92:1-2 says, "It is good to praise the Lord and make music to your name, O Most High, to proclaim your love in the morning and your faithfulness at night."

What are the virtues of Christian character that reflect the character of God? Humility, generosity, kindness, faithfulness and love are virtues that reflect the character of God. One other Christian virtue that we sometimes forget is the heart of thankfulness. Thankfulness is a very important virtue in our Christian life. As the Psalmist said, it is good to start a day with praise and thankfulness, instead of worry or complaining. As we arise in the morning, we can thank God for his love, and we should do so. This attitude of thankfulness to God assures us of a pleasant day. I guarantee you that it assures happiness throughout the day. As we end the day and get into bed, thank Him once again for the specific demonstrations of His faithfulness during the day.

I recommend cultivating the heart of thankfulness, the attitude of thanking! It will make our life much happier. I know that there are many things that hinder us to give thanks and could cause us to complain. It is all right to identify these problems or shortcomings. However, start a day first with thanks to God and give appreciation to your fellow workers, your family and to your friends no matter what pots up in the morning. One of the songs we love to sing is, "Count Your Blessings one by one. You will be amazed at how many blessings you actually have."

Thankfulness is an attitude, it is the recognition that God in his goodness and faithfulness has provided for us and cared for us - both physically and spiritually. Thankfulness is recognition that we are totally dependent upon Him- all that we have comes from God.

We have a tendency to look for the problem first and forget to say thank you. To supervisors and those who have many workers under you; it is my recommendation to you, first give appreciation before you ask your workers to perform other task. It will motivate them and it will make them work doubly hard for you. This is not just a managerial technique from a manual, but it should come from of the heart and it is an attitude. Most of all, it is the principle that the Bible teaches us.

William James said, "The deepest human need is the need of appreciation." Appreciation comes when we give thanks from the heart, and a thankful heart not only brings happiness to the one who thanks, but brings so much encouragement to others. With a thankful heart you can say one word of affirmation and it, then, becomes a compliment. Mark Twain said, "I can live for a month on a single word of praise. Give me a full sentence of praise, and I can live for six months!!

With kind words and affirmation, you can build up your employees, your spouse, your children and your colleagues. Solomon said, "An anxious heart weighs a man down, but a kind word will cheer up the person."

I want to borrow the story for the well known counselor, Gary Chapman. He told his counseling story in the book, "The Five Love Languages", and it follows;

When you show appreciation and give a compliment, express it in a simple way, a straightforward statement. When you do that, you will not just give encouragement, you will motivate others to love you more. There was a lady whose husband never acknowledged her request to paint their bedroom. She asked her husband again and again to paint their room. Though the husband nodded yes, he never painted that room. Instead, He would spend his time cleaning and waxing his car. The lady thought that they had a serious marital problem because she thought that her husband never cared about her. When she visited a counselor, she recounted the story about her husband and the unpainted room. The counselor asked, "Is he doing other things for you, for example, throwing out the trash, etc.?" The lady said, "Yes."

The counselor asked another question, "Does your husband know that the room needs to be painted?" The lady answered once again, "Yes." The counselor suggested, "Never asks your husband to paint the room again, just give your appreciation for whatever your husband does." The lady was unsettled by the guidance of the counselor, but she followed the counselor's advice anyway. A few months later, the lady called the counselor, "Your prescription worked amazingly!" When you express thanks to others, God and others will do more for you. (The Five Love Languages p.p. 40-41, Gary Chapman, Northfield Publisher)

Even at the time when Paul was writing his letters to his congregation in order to confront certain problems, he first praised and thanked to his congregation. "I always thank God for you, because of His grace given to you in Christ Jesus."(1st Corinthians chapter 1) This gesture was genuine and it came from his heart. That was one of the reasons why he was greatly used by God.

We are anxious to receive but are often too careless in giving thanks. We desperately pray to God for help in our crises in our lives, and then when God interventions and we receive what we need from God, we tend to forget the source of the blessing and proceed to praise ourselves rather than God for the good results. Look at the story of Luke 17:11-19, the account of the healing of the ten lepers. Here were ten men in the most pitiful of all human misery. Not only were they afflicted with a terrible and loathsome disease; but also they were outcasts from society because of their disease. Jesus healed them. As these men went to show themselves to the priest so that they could come back and accepted by their families and friends, only one of them, realizing what had happened, turned back to give thanks to Jesus. Ten men were healed, but only one gave thanks. Look at how he thanked to Jesus. He came back, praising God in a loud voice. He threw himself at Jesus' feet and thanked him. Interesting thing was that he was a Samaritan, not a Jew. Jesus was frustrated about the fact that only one person out of ten came to give thanks. He was more frustrated because no one from Jews came back for thanks. He asked, "Were not all ten cleansed? Where is the other nine? Was no one to be found to return and give praise to God, except this foreigner?"

It is very important to remember God's provision and thanking Him for the blessings we receive. It is also important to give thanks those who took care of us. As mother's day come, I want to urge you to give thanks to your moms. Not just on the mother's day, but every day. I want to read what Rev. Fred wrote for Mother's day. Here is the MOTHER'S DAY GREETING.

Happy Mother's Day! Mark Twain said, "With a One word compliment, I can live up to two months. So, if I receive six words of compliments, I can live up to one year!" One of the deepest desires of the humankinds is receiving rewards. Outwardly and inwardly one wants to feel appreciated. Children and husbands, think about your mother and mother of your children, give your appreciation to them. In modern day life, each day is busy and stressful. It is easy to forget your spouse's hard work to support you and to make the family harmonious. Often we take our mother's love for granted. So why not just say "thanks" once in a while. Even better to say, "I appreciate your---!"

Hundreds of Bible stories teach us this important fact. Thankfulness is very important in the practice of the Christian life. In Psalms, there are many songs of thanksgiving. Especially in Psalm 107, we can find the reasons for thanksgiving. It says, "Give thanks to the Lord, for He is good. His love endures forever. Let the redeemed of the Lord say this- those he redeemed from the lands, from the east and west, from the north to the south. Some wandered in desert wastelands, finding no way to a city where they could settle. They were hungry and thirsty, and their lives were ebbing away."

During the encampment in the wilderness of Sinai, the Lord became the guide, protector, the provider, and liberator of Israel. There was neither food, nor water in the desert. But, God led their way during the day with clouds and the fire at night. Whether we recognize or not, God' provision and guidance in our lives are same to us. The Psalmist continues: "God led them straight away to a city where they could settle. Let them give thanks to the Lord for His unfailing love and His wonderful deeds for men, for He satisfies the thirsty and fills the hungry with good things." In the desert, there were neither Restaurants, nor McDonald store. The Israelites just survived with the basic things. The supplies of meat and water were a constant problem. Still, throughout the history of their wanderings, the Israelites continuously learn to give thanks, not because of any fancy things God had given, but just because they had survived in the wilderness. Although they failed to do thanks sometimes, they had learned not just thankful for the water and the meat, but for God's unfailing love. The assurance of God's unfailing love was overwhelming in their hearts. With thanksgiving to God, they recognized that God in His goodness had provided and cared for them.

What is the purpose of thankfulness? The primary purpose of giving thanks to God is to acknowledge His goodness and to honor Him. In Psalm 50:23, God says, "He who sacrifices thank offerings, honors me." When we give thanks to the Lord, we proclaim His mighty acts; we acknowledge His goodness.

What is good about thanksgiving?

First, it gives us courage to face the problems that we are going through now : "Remembering God's previous mercies encourages us to trust Him for mercies we need today."

Second, thankfulness promotes contentment. Our true satisfaction does not come from our possessions, or our position. Satisfaction comes when we focus on God's providence. If our mind and our thoughts focus on the blessings God has already given, we could stop wasting our time for the yearning of things we do not have, or have lost.

Thirdly, thankfulness brings miracles. There is sometimes a situation where we do not necessarily want to be thankful. For instance, when Paul and Silla were preaching the gospel at the open market square at Philippi, a slave girl who performed Magic for the owner of a shop followed Paul and Silla and shouted to the people, "These men are servants of the Highest God, who are telling you the way to be saved. She kept up bothering and interrupting Paul's ministry for many days. Because of her interruption, Paul and Silla became troubled. All at once Paul turned around and commanded the evil spirit in the girl: "In the name of Jesus Christ I command you to come out of her." At that moment the spirit left her. And the owner who made lots of money by using this girl realized that he lost his big income source. The owner accused Paul and Silla and motivated our crowed to accuse them. So, the crowd attacked Paul and Silla. Paul and Silla ended up locked in the prison. The magistrate ordered them to be stripped and beaten. After they had been severely flogged, they were thrown into prison, and jailer was guard them carefully. They were hurled into an inner cell and had their feet fastened in stocks. This could have been a time when they could have had doubt in their mind: "What am I doing in here? We have done a lot for God; we proclaimed His gospel and worked hard for Him. But here we are now beaten, rejected and thrown into prison" They could complain and regretful. They could have worried, "Are we going to spend our life in this prison forever?" There was no promise of tomorrow for them. However, look at what they did. About the midnight Paul and Silla prayed and sang hymns to God. They prayed and sang so loudly that other prisoners listened to them. Then, look at what happened? Suddenly there was such a violent earthquake that the foundations of the prison were shaken. At once all the doors flew open, and everyone's chains were broken and they were released from the chain. (Acts 16:vs.16-38) Thanksgiving changed a perilous situation as a blessing. Thanksgiving brought miracles. Thanksgiving brought freedom. Thanksgiving brought a brighter future. With that experience, Paul urges us, that when we pray to God, include thanksgiving: "Do not be anxious about anything, but in everything, by prayer and petition, with thanksgiving present your requests to God." (Phil 4:6, 7)

Are you worried about something? Do you have doubt about tomorrow? Pray to God with thanksgiving. Thank God with the attitude that He has already answered you. Even though you cannot see the reality right now, view the future event as if it has already been accomplished in your favor and give thanks.

Let me conclude with the summary: Thank God, for it gives us courage to face each day with the memory of God's grace to us in the past, in the present and into the future. Thankfulness promotes our contentment and happiness; thankfulness brings miracles - all kinds of miracles. The ultimate miracle is that which brings the miracle of peace into our heart when nothing else can give us peace. Thanksgiving is a practice of new life of a good Christian. I pray that God would keep our mind filled with peace and joy by giving us the spirit of thanksgiving.

FORGIVE AS THE FATHER FORGIVES YOU
Luke 15:11-32, Matthew 18:21-35

Life is continues series of problem solving and this is a challenge to us. One of the biggest challenges is forgiving those who hurt us badly. But we have to forgive. Otherwise, there is much sadness and devastation because people cannot forgive other members of their family. If the rift occurs between father and mother, their children, it affect very seriously. I am now going to quote from part of a poem of youngster that was sent to Dr. James Dobson's 'Focus on the Family' program. It was such a touchy topic. "Does a child understand the gradual separation of a woman and man? Flashbacks haunt my thoughts- those scary, scary words. Why can't I just erase the threats I overheard? Mommy's body pushed; the vase that's on the floor; Mommy crying, in such a pain. Dad runs out the door. I'm frozen in the recurrent scene- No crying nor speaking - Why? I'm filled with fear and bad sorrow. But no tear slips from my eye." (Page 166, Dr. Dobson: "Turning Hearts toward the Home")

Forgiving! It is not the word to only apply in the relationship with other than the family. Forgiving is the word that should first apply in the family relationship. All make mistakes; all have gone astray; all have sinned. So, everyone hurts others, likewise, each one is hurt by others; spouse to spouse, brothers to brothers, sisters to sisters, parents to children, children to parents.

One of the most important traits in a healthy family is the ability to forgive for each other. It is very important to nurture forgiveness in family relationships. I have seen many people who have been hurt in the family relationship. Even in the family relationship, there still is a tension and negative dynamic, because everybody has a different character and personality.

Since human nature is less than perfect, we cannot expect to have a perfect relationship with other human beings, even within the realm of the family. In the first book of the Bible, the book of Genesis, we can see much torment in the family relationship. What was the first incidence of murder? Cain and Abel, who was first brother among human race, experienced the tragedy of murder. This kind of story kept on with Essau and Jacob, the brothers of Joseph.

What happened in Joseph's family? His brothers sold Joseph to foreigners as a slave. This kind of story continues until now. So, do not surprise when you get hurt in the family relationships. Conflict in the family is a common thing. But, the important thing in family relationships is that we can forgive each other. It is necessary to have a healthy family.

The Christian Bible is so influential, not because it records perfect human beings, but because it records openly the faults and weaknesses of people as well. The Bible also shows us how people become reconciled with each other.

For example, as you well know, twin brothers Jacob and Esau, had long period of conflict because they had to fight for the blessings of their father. They could not even remain together under the same roof. As a result, they had long 20 years of separation. However, after twenty years of hatred and separation, the brothers met once again. Esau ran to meet Jacob and embraced him; Esau threw his arms around Jacob's neck and kissed him. And both wept. Jacob thought that Esau still held great anger toward him and tried to pacify Esau with an offering of his property. But Esau said, "I already have plenty, my brother. Keep what you have for yourself." Jacob insisted on bestowing his favor on Esau and said. "Please, take my gift. I want to give it to you, because I have found favor in your eyes, and it seems to me that your face resembles the face of our gracious God." They forgave each other. (Genesis 35) It was a beautiful story of forgiveness and it should be emphasized not just as a family story but also as an integral part of the peace process concept in the Middle East nowadays.

Not long ago, one of the influential leaders of the Midwest passed away. He left a few parting words to his people and they were; "We have only one enemy. They are Israel people" His anger toward the Jews was very severe. Few years ago, a young Jewish man, who was a prospective and very well educated lawyer, not at all irrational, assassinated their prime minister. He assassinated the Israelites prime minister, because their prime minister had signed the peace treaty with the Arabs.

Both prejudiced men should have learned from Jacob and Esau's reconciliation, their forgiveness and love as brothers. Many people focus on the fact that Esau and Jacob fought. However, we have to focus on the fact that both brothers were finally able to reconcile and to forgive each other.

Later on in Genesis, there is a record of another beautiful story of forgiveness. As you know, Joseph experienced a hard life from the time he was teenager until he became a prime minister at age. 30. Joseph was once a slave, and at another time was a prisoner. He went through many difficulties, anguish and emotional turmoil. It was because his brothers had been jealous of Joseph and sold him to the merchant from Arabia.

When Joseph became the prime minister of Egypt, his brothers had to stand before him. Recognizing that a powerful man of the world, the prime minister of Egypt who stood right in front of them, was their brother, all of his brothers who had sold Joseph were afraid of the revenge Joseph might seek to levy. However, Joseph had already forgiven his brothers. In fact, Joseph could not control his emotion of compassion. He wept very loudly in front of them. Joseph was releasing all of the pain and suffering that he had endured in the past. As he wept, Joseph announced to his brothers, "I am Joseph! Is my father still living?" But his brothers were not able to answer him because they were still terrified at his presence. Joseph told them, "Come close to me. Do not be distressed and do not be angry with yourselves for selling me, because it was God who sent me ahead of you and has saved the world from hunger and has preserved the Israel tribe as a remnant on earth." (Genesis 45: 4-7) Joseph not only told them that he forgave them, but asked them to forgive themselves.

Physical and/or mental grief in the family make bruises more severe and make its scars deeper, because it happen between loved ones. Hatred is not the opposite of love. The opposite of love is the attitude of 'I Do Not Care'. A broken relationship, especially in the family relationship, brutalizes emotions and sometimes destroys life. This is because their loved one hurts their family more than others. If someone who was not close to us hurts us, the pain would not last long. So, forgivingness is the word that has to apply to the near family first, as the first book of the Bible showed us.

Malachi is the last prophet of the Old Testament who prophesied the coming of John the Baptist, the forerunner of the Son of God of our Lord Jesus Christ. He prophesied, "See, I will send the prophet Elijah before that great and dreadful day of the Lord comes. He will turn the hearts of the fathers, and the hearts of the children to their fathers." (Malachi 4:6)

Christ, who came after 400 years following the silent period, was sent as our reconciler. He came to this world to turn the hearts of mothers and fathers to their children and the hearts of the children to their parents. The parable of prodigal son gave us the great parable of the forgiving father. The prodigal son ran off to a far country and lived such a wild life. After he spent all of his money the son came back to the father. He did not look like the same son any longer. He wore ragged clothes and looked miserable. But while he was still a long way off, his father recognized him and was filled with compassion for him.

He ran to his son, threw his arms around him and kissed him. The son said to him, "Father, I have sinned against heaven and against you. I am no longer worthy to be called your son." The prodigal son couldn't expect to get back the son-ship of his father. He just wanted to live at his father's house and be fed. However, the father forgave the son and forgot all of his sins. This father was like a father in Psalm 103: 12-14, "As far as the east is from the west, so far has he removed our transgressions from us." The father said to his servants, "Quick! Bring the best robe and put it on him. Put a ring on his finger and sandals on his feet. Bring the fattened calf and kill it. Let us have a feast and celebrate. For this son of mine was dead and is alive again; he was lost and is found!" This father is our father in heaven and forgives our sin and asks us to forgive each other. Would you do the same thing to your blood? Now, we have a few more days of this year. If you haven't have chance to do reconcile with your kinsman, I encouraged picking up the phone and call and have a cheerful conversation with other, especially with your family members, do not wait for them to call you, you do it first. That is what we should do since we become changed as new loving, kind, and generous person.

Imitating Christ's Humility
Philippians 2:1-11

Paul addressed this message to his congregation as a principle of community life to teach how to live and work harmoniously. Because of our carnal human nature, there are many conflicts in the relation between human being. I've heard from one pastor who used to be a missionary and who is now a professor in a seminary. He said that, "When I did missionary work, there were conflicts between the workers, and so, I thought if I became a teacher, there would be no further conflicts between staff. But it was not true."

There are lots of good things going within the congregation of the Philippians' church: encouragement among its members and comfort for others demonstrated in love, tenderness and passion. However, in Paul's perspective, they missed one thing. It was the unity. They cannot be one. There were divisions among the church members. It was the same problem in the church of Corinth. One group said, "I belong to Paul", the other group said, "I am of Peter, the first apostle." Paul told them "Is Christ divided? Were you baptized in the name of Paul? Was Paul crucified for you? Why were there fractions, why were there divisions?" The root of the problem of division was a pride; vain conceit or self-ambition. Paul told them, "I plead with you, by the name of Jesus Christ, that you speak the same thing, and let there be no division among you. But you may be perfectly joined together in the same mind and the same judgment." Paul recited the same prayer to the church of Philippians. In verse three, Paul said, "If you have any encouragement from being united with Christ, if there is any comfort from His love, if there is any fellowship with the Spirit, if there is any tenderness and compassion, then make my joy complete by being like-minded, having the same love, being one in spirit and one in purpose."

How could they be united as one and have a harmonious ministry?

Paul now suggested humility as the basic principle of life by saying, "Be humble and do everything with an attitude of humility and regard others better than me in something." This means to respect and honor each other. This is the principle of a new life. In old days, you may be a person of puffed off, now as a new creature, you should live humble life.

I believe that we can apply this principle in the marriage relationship, in family life, as well as the principle for our work relationships. We can do all of those wonderful things of encouragement to others, fellowship with others, helping others and consolation in trials. The outcome of our efforts may look good on the surface. But if we do not do all of those wonderful things with humility, we are not doing as God wanted us to do.

What is humility? The dictionary meaning is "the state of being free from pride."

Jonathan Edwards, a famous preacher of the 17th Century, who started a great awakening movement, said,

"In our relationship with God, humility inclines us to distrust ourselves and depend only upon God. The proud person has a high opinion of his own wisdom or strength or righteousness and is inordinately self-confident. The humble person relies upon God and delight to cast themselves wholly on Him as their refuge and strength. In the human relationship, humility tends to prevent an inordinate aspiration to wealth or position and it prevents ambitious behavior among people. A humble person is content with his situation among others and remains tranquil, allowing God to direct him as God wishes. A humble person is not greedy for honor. Nor does he try to appear uppermost and exalted above his neighbors."

Humbleness before God will bring many fruits. Those fruits are service, submission and honor. I would like to speak about those three fruits very briefly.

First: Service. Jesus Christ knelt down as a servant and washed the dusty feet of His disciples at the night before He was betrayed and was crucified. Do you remember that unforgettable story? Of course, you do! Jesus, the King of kings humbled Himself and served.

Second: Submission. We often pray like this, "I pray that Your Will be done. But, I want to do this MY way." My brothers and sisters, I ask you first to give up your own will and submit to God's Will. Then, submit to each other. That may sound very difficult to do, but with the memory of Jesus' humility firmly implanted in our minds and hearts, we can submit to each other. And in that submission to each other we become a united, free from divisions and conflicts.

Third: Honor. Thomas A Campus, one of the saints from the middle Ages, declares in his book entitled, The Imitation of Christ : "Every man naturally desires to know. But, what does knowledge avails of itself without the fear of God? BETTER, surely, is a humble laborer who serves God, than a proud philosopher, who neglecting himself for studies the course of the heavens. The deepest and the most profitable lesson is this, which we quest for true knowledge with God as our center of focus. To have a healthy contempt of us, it is great wisdom and a high level of perfection to esteem nothing of ourselves and always think others as higher person. If you should see another openly sin, or see that person commit some heinous offense, you ought not to esteem yourself the better person. You know not how long you shall be able to remain in good standing. Nor should you judge another, because you have no idea of the background that provoked that person to sin or commit that offence. All of us are frail, but you ought to think of yourself as the frailest of all." He was mainly asking us to give honor and respect to others.

Service, submission, honor are the fruits of the humility that the Holy Spirit makes possible with our cooperation. As Christians, we are required to imitate Christ. As followers of Christ, we are required to have Christ-like humility.

Paul gives us a profound lesson about humility at Philippians 2: 5-8. In this passage there are two basic lessons of humility.

1. Humility means humanity

Jesus emptied Himself of His God nature; He emptied His mind of His supernatural gifts and regarded Himself as nothing. Jesus assumed the role of a human. A good expression in English is that "Jesus was a down to the earth" man.

Modern Psychology helps people by raising their self-esteem, which I think is a good trend. However, we must also learn to empty our minds as well. We must not be self-centered with a feeling of pride. We must empty our minds of this pride. We are mere humans. Spurges, the English Minister from the Nineteenth Century, describes this truth very beautifully when he gave his Christmas sermon, " The creator of the universe and all the beautiful stars in the heaven, the eternal God whose hair is gray and white as snow, now grasped the bosom of Mary, a mere human, to get His nourishment."

2. God exalted Jesus highly.

When we humble ourselves, we are afraid of perishing or dying in the estimation of others. But, Remember, God did not let Jesus perish. While hanging on the cross and finally succumbing to death, it appeared that Jesus was lost and totally rejected by the onlookers. Yet, we know that Jesus was resurrected from the dead and exalted as the ruler over all people. This humble God/Man became the most honored of all men.

God will bless those who are humble and meek. Jesus said on the Sermon on the Mount, "Blessed are those who are meek!" In the Old Testament, there are many scriptures that tell us how God esteems the humble person.

Isaiah 57:15 say, "For this is what the high and lofty One says- He who lives forever, whose name is holy; 'I live in a high and holy place, but also with him who is contrite and lowly in spirit.'"

Isaiah 66: 1-2 say, "This is what the Lord says; 'Heaven is my throne and the earth is my footstool. Where is the house you will build for Me? Where will my resting place be? Has not My Hand made all these things, and so they came into being, declares the Lord. This is the one I esteem; he who is humble and contrite in spirit, and trembles at My Word."

Proverbs 22:4 say, "Humility and the fear of the Lord bring wealth and honor and life." The Bible warns strongly against pride as the start of the fall. The Bible blesses humbleness as the beginning of honor and abundant life. We should learn from Christ's humility since we became new born again Christian. Then, people will know that we are changed and it will bless our life.

Love your neighbor: Who is your neighbor?
Luke 10: 25-37

Since Christ's parable of the Good Samaritan is so famous, I do not have to tell this story in detail. However, it has a profound teaching that we have to think it over and over again. In this parable, Jesus Christ poses one important question to us, "Who is the neighbor?" Who is going to help you at the moment when you face tragedy? When you see others who meet tragedy, are you going to be their 'neighbor', just like a Good Samaritan? I am so glad that our church could support the Romanian youth mission. Our community sent twenty-eight youth to help the homeless and poverty-stricken people in Romania. I appreciate these twenty-eight young adults, who donated their spring vacation to be "the neighbor" of those whom they had never met and whom they did not know. Let us become a good neighbor like them to each other. Then, we will experience a heaven in this earth. New way of living God's life is to extend your neighbor to all people, although they are different than you and love them as neighbor.

Let me introduce one of the interpretations of Christ's parable of the Good Samaritan. There was a brilliant scholar in the early age of the church named St. Augustine. He offered an allegorical interpretation of the Good Samaritan. Please give your attention and connect St. Augustine's interpretation with Jesus' parable of the Good Samaritan. You are invited to give your opinion in the interpretation of St. Augustine. Try to see how each phrase has a mystical significance.

- A Certain man: humankind

- Went down from Jerusalem: Jerusalem means the heavenly city of peace. So, this phrase means that humankind fell and kicked out from heaven and fell as this troubled world.

- Jerico: Jerico means the moon, thereby signifying Adam's mortality---After Adam had sinned and had fallen, he had to leave paradise and go down to the place of death and mortality.

- There were Thieves: meaning the devil and his evil angels were there.

- They stripped him: meaning that the man was stripped of his immortality. He basically lost eternal life and was destined to die.

- They beat him: In other words it means to persuade the man to sin.

- Left him half-dead: These words show that although a man lives physically, if he is dead spiritually, the man is therefore, half-dead.

- The priest and Levite: signify the priesthood and ministry of the Old Testament.

- The Samaritan: He worked untiringly to save a man he did not know. So, the Samaritan means Christ himself.

- Bound his wounds: It means binding the restraint of sin

- The Samaritan used oil: It means comfort and hope

- The Samaritan gave the man wine: an exhortation to work with a fervent spirit

- The man is placed on the donkey: interpreted also as the flesh of Christ's incarnation.

- The inn: is the Church

- Next day: the time after the resurrection

- Two silver coins: show a promise of this life and the life to come

- The innkeeper: signifies Paul

With this allegorical interpretation of the parable of the Good Samaritan, St. Augustine laid the ground of his doctrine of salvation. This doctrine matches perfectly with our belief. Many Presbyterians buys this allegorical interpretation. They preached, "We were like the man who was stripped and beaten and left half dead because of our sin. Jesus Christ, our Savior and our true Neighbor, showed mercy on us like a Good Samaritan." I believe that is the wonderful message.

Now let me introduce different interpretation of this parable. Baptists say that this story has no need of allegorical interpretation. Baptists believe that they just have to comprehend the point what Jesus was trying to make through the story. Their recommendation for the correct interpretation is to place yourself in the context of the story and discover main point and bring it into your life and simply ask question, 'what does it mean to you?' For the Baptists, the main task for the interpretation of the Samaritan story is to discover who is your neighbor and once you determine who your neighbor is, to love them as the Good Samaritan did. I believe both St. Augustine and the Baptists have valid interpretation. Since we already examined the view of the Augustinians, now let us examine this story with the Baptists' view.

The first character of this drama was a man, not a Jew or other specified person. He wore no badge, no identification of any nation or social group and he did not even carry any religious identification. He was just a man, which means he was one of humankind. So, this man could be any of us. And because of the nature of life, we are exposed to the danger of becoming a victim like this man every day.

Who was the first man to come down and saw this tragedy? It was the priest. Priests had to pass this road each week after their service in the Temple. After serving God for a week, this priest was encountered with an excellent opportunity of serving man. However, the situation was very complicated for the priest, because he could not find the identity of the man who suffered the tragedy. Since the priest had no way to figure it out about the beaten man' social position and religious affiliation, the priest could not discover whether this man was a Jew or a Samaritan or one who came from some other nation. To this priest, this man did not look like a Jew. Furthermore, he could not determine whether this man was dead or alive. If he touched the body of dead person, he could defile himself. I am sure that he thought about, 'What is the best way. If I stay here and try to help him, I could be hurt or defile him.' He concluded that he had to get away from that situation. He talked to himself, 'Do not involve these uncertain things and stay far away from the situation as possible.'

Second man who came down to this road was a Levite, who was a helper of the priest. He had same opinion with the priest. Both the priest and the Levite regarded highly the word of God which said, 'Love the Lord your God with all your heart and with all your soul and with all your strength and with your entire mind' and 'Love your neighbor as yourself'. It was mentioned in the Bible long time ago. Leviticus 19:18 says, 'Love your neighbor as yourself.' I want to point out that this was taught as the Jewish ethic from the Old Testament ages. Lawyers, priests and Jewish knew well this scripture and regarded the love of neighbor as their highest moral value.

But the problem of leaders in the Old Testament was that they limited "neighbor" only to their own tribes. In the story of Good Samaritan, even though the priest and the Levite had learned and preached to love their neighbors as themselves, when they met this great tragedy, they had no guilt feeling to pass by because they would simply say to themselves, "Since this man is not my neighbor. I have no obligation to him and I have other priorities, which is to love my fellow law keepers and to love my brother Jews." In this parable, the Jewish religious leaders definitely excluded other races and people who practiced other religions. To the Jews, a lack of love is not mainly caused by the lack of pity for the man facing the tragedy, but mainly caused by the "concept of neighbor" in their legalistic and nationalistic attitude.

Jesus was confronting this people with the story of Good Samaritan to change their concept of the neighbor. With the parable of the Good Samaritan, Jesus Christ confronted them and asked the question, "Which of these three do you think was a neighbor to the man who fell into the hands of the robbers?" With this question, Jesus exposed the prejudice and the hatred they held in their hearts. When confronted by Christ, the Levite lawyer and the Priest had no way to justify their actions, nor could they run away. Christ forced them to answer, 'Who is the neighbor of this person?' They answered, "The one who had mercy on him." Jesus' response to them was, "Go and do likewise"

Obey your parents
Ephesians 6: 1-4

In the teaching of the Lord's Prayer, Jesus Christ taught us to pray to the Father in heaven saying, 'Our Father Who art in heaven.' When we pray, we call upon our ' Heavenly Father ', a phrase that is so common and natural nowadays. We automatically call our Lord, 'Father'. However, during those days when Christ lived in Jewish society, referring to God as 'The Father' was a very radical expression. People thought of God as only a spiritual and fearful supreme being; they would never dare to approach God on such an intimate basis. In those days, if one approached God and referred to God on a personal level without the appropriate stature or holiness they could possibly be condemned. However, Christ emphasized the nearness of God, using such affirmations as 'Father.' In the New Testament we are even taught that we can call God "Abba, Father". Abba, Father has a similar connotation calling God as "Daddy".

Holy Scripture teaches us many things that God provides for us as our heavenly Father. It is very beneficial to observe the fatherly duties of our Lord, which are outlined in the Bible, because it reminds us of God's fatherly love and demonstrates to us the relationship of parents with their children.

God the Father in Heaven provides and nurtures us. In the Sermon on the Mount, Jesus Christ said that God as our Father feeds and clothes us. Jesus said, "Look at the birds of the air; they do not sow or reap or store away in barns, and yet your heavenly Father feeds them. Are you not much more valuable than they?" (Matthew 6:26)

With this scripture I want to address two important things to you.

First of all, the Heavenly Father nurtures and feeds us through our parents.

Second, parents are the representation of our heavenly Father even though they are not perfect like God. Their love, concern and care are the represents God's fatherly love to their children. So, if we do not give proper respect and honor to our parents and yet we say that we still love our Father in heaven, God would remind us that one must first learn to respect and honor one's visible parents. That is what the apostle Paul is saying this morning to you. "Children, obey your parents in the Lord, for this is right action. Honor your father and mother, which is the first commandment with additional promise; 'that it may go well with you and that you may enjoy long life on the earth.'" In Paul's recommendation of the relationship with the parents and the children, he first started to speak about what children supposed to do with regard to their parents. Children need to learn to obey and honor their parents. Proverbs 6:20-23 states, "My son, keep your father's commands and do not forsake your mother's teaching and bind them upon your heart forever. Fasten them around your neck. When you walk, they will guide you and when you sleep, they will watch. When you awake, they will speak to you. For these commands are a lamp; this teaching is a light and the correction of discipline are the ways to life."

Who are the fathers and/or mothers that we should honor and obey?

In a broad sense, parents are those who raise us: good politicians like the father of our country; schoolteachers; ministers. Most of all, God's given relationship with physical parents and children is very special relationship. During the process of my adolescence, I thought that I was brought up purely by my own ability. So, whenever my parents' advice differed from my way of thinking, I thought, 'They are old fashioned; I will do things my own way.' I did not fully recognize the efforts and care and love that my parents were consistently giving to me. After I grew into adulthood and became a parent for my own children, I started to recognize efforts as well as cares of my parents.

I first want to remark that the Ten Commandments of Moses are still valid commandments, because Christ regards them highly. Among those commandments, four are related to God and our relationship with Him. The remaining six address human beings and their relationships with each other, whether it is parents/ children, women/ men, neighbor. Among those remaining commandments, the only commandment that holds a promise is the one that states that we must honor our parents. Deuteronomy 5: 16 tell that this commandment has the promise of a blessing. This commandment also tells that there will be a strong punishment if children do not obey and honor their parents. (Mark 7: 10-12)

The second remark that I would care to make is that God in heaven will take care of your children as if they are His own and we can entrust our children to HIM. Every parent wants to nurture and support their children as best as they can. However, since parents are also human. The have limitations because they are not perfect beings. So, sometimes they may feel that they are inadequate as parents. But remember, God is your children's perfect Father. Although you cannot perfectly take care of them, God will complete in taking care of your children when you do best to care of your children in your part. God will continue to take care of your children perfectly into eternity as their eternal Father.

God does, as our Father, sometimes discipline us. Just as the heavenly Father disciplines, as parents we need the fortitude to guide our children in the right path. Parents are duty-bound and must take on the responsibility of maintaining all of the commandments in their own lives and in the lives of their children. Parents have to give respect to their children as well. There is no wavering, no bending, and no exceptions to the rules.

The third remark that I want to make is that the parents should give respect to their children as well. The significant difference between the Ten Commandments and Oriental teaching in regard human relationship is that the relationship the oriental philosophy is one way and authoritative but Christianity teaches that a relationship should be two ways. Children must respect their parents, but parents should respect their children as well. The scripture of Ephesians chapter 6:4

said, "Father, do not exasperate your children; instead bring them up in the training and instruction of the Lord." If the father does not take care of his children, it will hurt their personality and affect their whole response to life even after they are grown. So, parents have to give full and equal respect to their youngsters and to their children just as the children must give respect to parental authority. One of the parental authorities that the children should accept is the righteous discipline from their parents because if parents just spoil their children, children will go the wrong way. Good discipline and good teaching and the commandments are the lamp and the light and the way to a blessed life. Just as an aside, discipline should come from love, not hatred and discipline should be conducted not through emotional status, but reasonable manner.

In conclusion, allow me to say that God's love for us is best described as a parental love and parents are the representative of God's fatherly love to their children and the love relationship between parents and the children are heavenly Father's unique blessing to our humankind. Parents who teach good ethics and faith to their children as an inheritance will harvest their children as their crown. Children who respect and obey their parents will be blessed. In old days you may not give full respect and honor to your parents, now since you are born anew, you will honor your parents, most of all, God the heavenly Father.

Focus on the future goal
Philippians 3:12-21

This letter that Paul addressed to the Philippians will be a very meaningful message for us today in our first worship service of the year. A new year is always exciting because it allows us to dream anew and to set new goals. Today's passage tells us three things for us to start a new year positively. I want to challenge you with Paul's message to the Philippians to get a new feeling, to breathe the new air of the New Year.

1. We should have a goal for this year.
2. We should have a humble attitude.
3. We should look forward to the future.

I. Toward the goal of life

Do you have a goal for this year or are you just going to live an extension of last year? Are you still living in the past? To succeed in life, we must first set up our goal. Today is the first day of the rest of our life. Apostle Paul exhorts us to 'press toward the goal to win the prize'. No doubt Paul is one of the greatest figures in Christian history who lived successfully in the history. Why was he successful? He was successful because he had a goal. When Paul wrote the Philippians Epistle, he was already a matured old man. His spiritual son Timothy was grown up and became a pastor of his own flock. Furthermore, Paul was in prison and faced a trial that could end up the life as a criminal. Think about it- Paul was in prison when he said 'I have a goal for my life'. If Paul in his situation could have a goal for his life, how much more could we, who are free, have a goal? Someone might say, "Setting a goal! I had done many times. It just makes me frustrated because I realized that I failed to accomplish every year." However, making a goal motivates you to try again and it gives purpose of your life.

II. Humble attitude of life

Apostle Paul had the gray hair with his wisdom. He was a matured and well-knowledgeable Christian when he said in verse 12, 'I do not say that I have at this time grasped the meaning of Christ, or that I have already become perfect in my knowledge of Him. But I keep pressing on to apprehend Christ Jesus.'

As you already know, Paul wrote most of the epistle in the New Testament- over half of the New Testament. He is the one who established the ground of Christian Theology, yet he said, 'I indeed apprehended him not'. He should be the one who could say 'I fully apprehend Christ'. Yet he realized that he had not grasped the meaning of Christ and he said, 'I had not fully apprehend and need to grow more'. It was a humble and honest confession of the old man. That was why he still had room to grow and he still had hope for the future. He still had excitement for the dream that he was awaiting. He still enjoyed learning. All this is summed up in his statement, 'I do not say that I have at this time grasped the meaning of Christ'. This is the final words of the greatest Christian who ever lived, spoken in the face of death concerning his unquenchable spiritual desire to learn more about Christ. This desire is seen in the words of the song 'More About Jesus'. Listen to the words:

More about Jesus let me learn

More, more about Jesus More of His saving fullness

See more of His love who died for me.

III. Forget what is behind and look forward to the future

To live this New Year successfully, we first need to forget what is behind and look forward to the future. We need to look ahead and not dwell in the past. We have a tendency to remember what we have to forget and forget what we have to remember. Paul's attitude leads us to success because He could say that 'to forget what is behind and stretch out to what lies before'. Regretting could be the opportunity to see you in the past mirror. But if we let regret fills us with remorse and it would limit our ability of do new things in the future. Then, we are not living in the present time. We cannot relive the past. I wish I could relive my youth, but I couldn't. So, just use the past as a mirror and tell your junior how to have a better life with lessons you've learned from the past failure. Most of all, we should live in the present time and look forward to the future.

Paul said in verse 16, "In any case, let us live up to whatever truth we have already attained'.(NIV) New King James Version make me to understand this verse more clearly, "To the degree that he have already attained, let us walk by the same rule." Either failure or success, we Christians should live up to whatever we have already attained. The reality of the present situation, whatever it is, is always the starting point and the ground that we can stand upon. We can't do anything about the past days- we can't correct, change, and add to those things already happened. But the future, which is before us, is a field of possibility that we can create a new history.

To look forward to the future, we need to look everything in God's perspective

God, as the One who sovereigns our life, has intervened in our lives and has led us to the present situation in whatever areas of your life; marriage, career, family, location, and friendship. We have to trust that God is the one who leads our life to the present time and unto this situation.

Have you heard the word "Ebenezer"? You can find this word at 1st Samuel 7:10-12. It is the word composed by two meaning, which are 'Help' and 'Stone'. It was a remark that was inscribed on the stone. Samuel inscribed 'Ebenezer' when the Israelites had victory at the battle with the Philistines. And it means "Thus far has the Lord helped us". Let me tell you this story briefly. Samuel had dual role both as judge and the prophet. He was a political and religious leader at the same time. While he was sacrificing the burnt offering, the Philistines sneaked in and came close to engage the Israel in the battle, but the Lord thundered in the loud thunder against the Philistines. The soldiers of Israel rushed out at Mizpeh and pursued the Philistines along the way to a point below Bethcar and they had won the war there. After this victory, Samuel took a stone and set it up between Mizpah and Bethcar and named it as "Ebenezer", which means, "thus far Yahweh has helped us." Samuel acknowledged that God led them to victory. It was a very great event. It was not so difficult to admit that God's sovereignty was present at the time of victory. However, we have to admit God's sovereignty even at the time of lost because God is the one who guide us whether in our success or defeat.

Because Paul acknowledged the divine guidance for him, he could release him from the past and look toward the future and could press forward to the goal. He says, "I press on toward the goal". Another translation of this verse is, "I keep running toward the goal marker, straight for the prize to which God called me to get the prize that is contained in Christ Jesus." The Sun of this New Year rose already. With the great expectation, hope, excitement, and freshness, let us run the track of this New Year. Take off all the burden of regret or pride of old year. Let us allow God to release from the past, work on your new days, and look up to the prize that is stored in heaven. Let us live a new life that has a goal in God.

COMMIT THY WAY TO THE LORD
Psalm 37: 1-7

In Psalm 37: 3-7, there are important principles that we can apply when we make decisions for life. Let us listen to these words prayfully, "Trust in the Lord and do good; dwell in the land and enjoy safe pasture. Delight yourself in the Lord and He will give you the desires of your heart. Commit your way to the Lord; trust on Him and He will do this: He will make your righteousness shine like the dawn, justice like the noonday sun. Be still before the Lord and wait patiently for Him." This Psalm gives principles of life.

First Principle: Do Good, Then Dwell in the Land and get blessing to enjoy a safe pasture

Sometimes we wonder why the other people, who were not honest before God and commit wrong actions prosper more than the person, who is sincere and honest. Psalm 10: 1-5 said, "Why, O Lord, do you stand far off? Why do you hide yourself in times of trouble?" In his arrogance the wicked man hunts down the weak, which are caught in the schemes he devises. He boasts of the craving of his heart; he blesses the greedy and reviles the Lord. In his pride the wicked does not seek God; in all his thoughts there is no room for God. But his ways are always prosperous." When we look at the unfairness and injustice, we are discouraged. These injustices discourage us continue to do good acts. However, if we realize that God's goodness rewards those who do good deed and trust Him, we can continue to do good act. Psalmist says that 'I am going to continue to do good deeds and I am always happy.' Psalmist recommends us "Trust in the Lord and do good; dwell in the land and enjoy safe pasture." Remember always that God is the one who sovereigns the world with His goodness. That guarantees our safety and insures an enjoyable life. The life of the man of Faith says that eventually the person who did good get the amazing rewards from God who is the source of blessing. As an example, I want to tell you about the life of Enoch. In Hebrew, it said, "Enoch was commended as one who pleased God." In his lifetime, Enoch had so much suffering; he hardly received any recognition, instead he experienced much persecution. However, God recognized Enoch and commended him as one who pleased God and took Enoch to heaven. Enoch did not even experience the pain of death when he was about to depart this world. So, the author of Hebrews recommends having faith like this, "Without faith, it is impossible to please God, because anyone who comes to Him must believe that He exists and the He rewards those who honestly seek Him." (Hebrews 11: 6) Our God, who is good exists and reins the world and history. He rewards those who do good deed.

Rewards come in many ways. God could reward us with material blessings, but it is not always materialized. It could be inward affirmation first; However, His rewards are greater than any other rewards.

Remember what the Lord said to Abraham in Genesis 15: 1 "Do not be afraid, Abram, I am your shield, your great reward." As we prepare for the upcoming year, I want to remind you that God is good, so it is a great wisdom to do good acts. One of the ways to do good is plant good seed of Gospel, live as a good Samaritan to your neighbor. You may not get the benefit right away, yet God who is good surely gives you the eternal rewards. The wisdom word said, "Cast your bread upon the waters, for many days you will find it again." When we do good deed in this world, it seems like we are throwing bread into the water just to see the bread sink. But someday, you will find your bread. When you bless others, that blessing will return to you. When he blesses open the floodgates of heaven and pour out so much blessing, it will be amazingly abundant." (Malachi 3: 10) It will be totally and permanently 100 percentages blessing.

Second Principle: Delight yourself in the Lord and believe that your hope and wishes would come true.

Most assuredly, God will give you the desires of your heart. Every human being has desires in their heart. We all human have every right to pursue happiness. I am certain that as we start this New Year we all are making fine wishes for the New Year. Christian faith supports those good wishes; of course, if those desires do not offend God's will or the desires aren't from ones greediness. As we sing, I do wish that you and your families have a very Happy New Year and that all of you to achieve the desires of your heart in the New Year. Just delight in the Lord and God will satisfy the desire of your heart. (Verse 4)

Third Principle: Commit your way to the Lord

Commit your way to the Lord and Trust in Him and He will make your righteousness shine like the dawn, and the justice of your will shall make you like the noonday sun. Wisdom word says, "Trust in the Lord with all your heart and lean not on your own understanding; in all your ways acknowledge him, and he will make your paths straight."(Proverbs 3:5-7)

Like sheep, we always need the shepherd's guide. We want to know which direction is toward peace and abundant life. In order to make good choice, we use our knowledge, experience, and our understanding. However, sometimes it is not easy to acknowledge which direction is the best way for achieving peace and life. In those conflicting times, we must continue to trust in the Lord, lean on Him and commit our direction to the Lord. In other words, we must acknowledge God' presence and the guide in all things.

Nothing in our life happens as an accident. You encounter people and experience some events because God plan for you with good intention. Be mindful of God's presence and follow the path that Jesus would lead you. Romans 11:33 says, "Oh, the depth of the riches of the wisdom and knowledge of God; How unsearchable His judgments and His paths beyond tracing out"

The encouraging word is in Psalm 37 verses 23, 24: "If the Lord delights in your way, he makes his steps firm; though he stumble, he will not fall, for the Lord upholds him with his hand." Who would fall if the strong and might Lord's hand uphold? Who would astray if God lead with His unsearchable wisdom?

Fourth Principle: Be still before the Lord

Sometimes, we couldn't do anything about the situation. At that time, all we could do is just waiting patiently. On those days, just be still before the Lord. Just step back and watch what the Lord is doing. If the Lord delights in your way, He makes your steps firm. If the Lord delights in your way, you will not fall even though you may stumble, because the Lord upholds you with His mighty and graceful Hand. Reinhold Niebuhr prayed in his famous serenity prayer that: "God! Grant me the serenity to accept the things I cannot change; courage to change the things I can; and wisdom to know the difference."

It is my prayer for you to be ready for the great new year! Give your good wishes to the Lord. Live a new life. Do good deed. Commit thy way to the Lord and be still in the Lord. Then, God will bless you make your life righteous and shine like the dawn in the morning and the noonday light.

Key verses:

"Trust in the Lord and do good; dwell in the land and enjoy safe pasture. Delight yourself in the Lord and He will give you the desires of your heart. Commit your way to the Lord; trust on Him and He will do this: He will make your righteousness shine like the dawn, justice like the noonday sun. Be still before the Lord and wait patiently for Him."

1. Conditional blessing: If you do this, then

One condition: Trust

Pairing Scriptures in the New Testament: 4: 6 "Do not be anxious about anything, but in everything, by prayer and petition, with thanksgiving, present your request to God.

Then, Blessing of Peace will be in your heart and minds.

- Trust
- Do Good
- Commit your way to

- Be Still

What does it mean "Trust in the Lord"?

What does it mean "Commit Thy way to the Lord"?

Then, Blessings comes in the New Days

- Verse 3: Dwell in the land and enjoy safe pasture
- Verse 6: Your righteousness shines like the dawn, justice like the noonday sun.
- Psalm 37 verses 23, 24: "If the Lord delights in your way, he makes his steps firm; though he stumbles, he will not fall, for the Lord upholds him with his hand."

Lord, Give Your Servant a Discerning Heart
1st Kings 3:1-15

How do we get wisdom?

First, as Solomon prayed humbly and asked God, who is the source of wisdom. When God offered to Solomon that He would give anything Solomon asked, he asked for the wisdom by asking to God, "I am but a little child; I do not know how to go out or come in. Give thy servant, therefore, an understanding mind that I may discern between good and evil."

Second, Ask God, the Holy Spirit to come into your heart and joins your inner spirit with the Spirit of God because Spirit of God draws the deep wisdom that dwells in God. As it said in the Bible, 'The Spirit searches all things, even the deep things of God, for who among men knows the thoughts of a man except the man's spirit within him.' (1st Corinthians 2: 10-12) In old days, you may lean just on your strength, but you rely one God everything and put God in your plan, since you are new person.

The Books of Job, Proverbs, and Ecclesiastes, along with few Psalms, are the product of what has been called the Hebrew wisdom literature. In ancient times wisdom was so important that the prophets and other counsels of nations closely worked with the leaders to give wisdom for the leaders when they needed to decide important issues. Wise kings listened to the prophets, but stubborn kings did not listen to the prophets. In the case of King Josiah, the whole country faced a national crisis, because Josiah did not listen to the prophet. Jeremiah prayed very essential and fundamental prayer for His nation and for the people. He prayed that "The law shall not perish from the priest, or the counsel from the wise, or the word from the prophet." (Jeremiah 18:18)

In these information ages, people regard knowledge as the most important matter. However, they do not realize how important the wisdom is. I agree that the knowledge is very important because many things that we are enjoying now are the products of the development of human knowledge. If someone did not invent the motor vehicle, we would not be able to arrive quickly to worship today.

We give high value to those who have knowledge. However, when there is something that we cannot resolve with our intellectual knowledge, we look for wisdom. We ask the question "Why?" or "How?" Wisdom has the answers.

Not all wise men are necessarily educated people. Knowledge comes from education, but wisdom comes from God. James said, "If any of you lacks wisdom, let him ask God, who gives all men generously and without reproach, and it will be given to him." (James 1:5) "Every good endowment and every perfect gift is from above, coming from the Father of lights with whom there is no variation or shadow to change." (James 1:17)

Here is a situation that calls for wisdom. There were two harlots who came to King Solomon for his fair judgment. In those days, the king acted as a judge, along with his other duties. One of the women said, "Oh, Lord, this woman and I dwell in the same house; and I gave birth to a child while she was in the house. Then, on the third day after I was delivered, this woman also gave birth; and we were alone; there was no one else with us in the house. And this woman's son died at midnight, because she laid on it. And she arose at midnight, and took my son from beside me, while your maidservant slept, and laid it on her bosom. When I rose in the morning to nurse my child, behold, it was dead, but when I looked at it closely in the morning, behold, it was not the child that I had borne. But the other woman said, "The living child is mine, and the dead child is yours." The first woman said, "No the dead child is yours, and the living child is mine." (1 Kings 3:16-28)

Without looking at the Bible, how do you think you would judge this case? If it happened nowadays, we could examine the DNA of the women and the baby to find out whose baby it was. But it was not possible in those days. With deep insight and an understanding of human nature, nature of the mother and the nature of love, Solomon found a way to judge this case and decide to whom the baby belonged. The King said, "Bring me a sword." The King wielded the sword and said, "Divide the living child in two, and give half to the one, and half to the other." Then the woman whose son was alive said to the King, because her heart yearned for her son, "Oh, My Lord, give her the living child". But the other woman said, "It shall be neither mine nor yours, divide it." At that moment the King answered and said, "Give the living child to the first woman."

In this case Solomon showed his great wisdom. All of Israel heard of the judgment, which the King had rendered; and they stood in awe of the King because they perceived that the wisdom of God was in the King to render justice. What is the wisdom of the Solomon? It was the understanding of a situation and the hearts of human beings and God. He measured correctly. Wisdom is also the ability to discern between good and evil.

Job 28:20 says, "Where then does wisdom come from? Where does understanding dwell? It is hidden from the eyes of every living being, concealed even from the birds of the air. God understand the way to it and he alone knows where it dwells, for He views the ends of the earth and sees everything under the heavens. When he established the force of the wind and measured out the waters, when he made a decree for the rain and a path for the thunderstorm, then he looked at wisdom and appraised it; he confirmed it and tested it, and he said to man, "The fear of the Lord- that is wisdom, and to shun evil is understanding." (Job 28: 20-28)

The proverb say, "Blessed is the man who finds wisdom, the man who gains understanding, for she is more profitable than silver and yields better returns than gold. She is more precious than rubies; nothing you desire can compare with the wisdom. Long life is in her right hand; in her left hand are riches and honor. Her ways are pleasant ways, and all her paths are peace. She is a tree of life to those embrace her; those who lay hold of her will be blessed." (Proverbs 3: 13-18) Proverb also recommends, "My son, preserve sound judgment and discernment, do not let them out of your sight; they will be life for you, an ornament to grace your neck."(Proverbs 3: 21-22)

Live by the Spirit
Zechariah 4: 1-14

The book of Zechariah is one of the "Apocalyptic literatures" It is similar with Revelation and the book of Daniel. Because of the nature of the "Apocalyptic" style, this book contains myriad of dreams and visions. In modern mentality, interpreting the dreams seems a little unrealistic. Yet, there is something hidden secret in each dream and in each vision. There is great benefit to unveil those meanings and find the treasure of the literature to comprehend God's revelation for our lives.

Nowadays, as a rule, the general Christian population gives little credence to dreams, I mean, real visionary dreams. For the most part I agree with the opinion that we cannot depend too heavily on dreams to discern God's will. Nonetheless, God sometimes reveals His will and vision for us through our dreams. In the days of the Old Testament, the interpretation of dreams was more prevalent. Joseph, Abraham, Jacob, and Daniel, all our great spiritual ancestors received a revelation in a dream. Now, in the dream within this passage, Zechariah saw something strange; the Angel woke him up just like someone who woke him up while he was in a sleep. The question of the angel was this, "What do you see?" This is a very important question for everybody to answer, because we see what we concerns. What we see makes us focus on that topic every day. For example, when Peter focused on Jesus who was walking on the sea, Peter joined Him and also walked on the water, although there was a storm all around him. When Peter focused on Jesus and saw Him, he remained peaceful and was never shaken. Peter stood tall and calm. However, as soon as Peter took off his gaze from Jesus and started to look at the storm and the strong wind around him, he immediately sank.

There were also many storms and noise around Zechariah's life that pulled off His focus to God. This turmoil prevailed amid a backdrop of Israelites who just had been released from the tyranny of Babylonian empire. The Israelites started immediately to rebuild their lives by first building their temple. There was much ridicule and frequent interruptions by those who objected to these Israelites who wanted to restore their center of faith.

There was particular frustration and doubt in the mind of the prophet, Zechariah. As I mentioned earlier, at the moment of Zechariah's despair, an angel woke him up, all within his dream, and the angel challenged Zechariah to focus on a vision from God. The angel asked, "What do you see?" As I stand before you, I too want to ask you and myself the same question, "What do you see? Do you see only the storms and the winds of life or hope?"

Like a man who had just awakened from sleep, Zechariah tried to focus on the vision that God had shown to him in his dream. Truly, it was a mystical dream. He saw, "A solid gold lamp stand with a bowl at the top and seven lights on the bowl with seven channels to the light. Also there are two olive trees alongside the lamp stand, one on the right of the bowl and the other on its left." The prophet was puzzled by the sight of this vision of a golden lamp stand and asked the angel, "What are these, my Lord?" The answer was not given immediately. In due course, however, God showed Zechariah the complete picture of the vision and answered part of its meaning.

The vision unfolds.

There were two gold pipes that pour out golden oil. Around the rim of this bowl, there are seven smaller bowls, each with seven pinches in the rim to hold seven wicks, making a total of forty-nine lights. On each side of the main bowl, there is a living olive tree with a branch overshadowing the bowl. So, the oil from each olive tree is fed directly through the golden pipe which provides the fuel to light up the lamp stand. What does this mean? The lamp stand represents Israel, which is the covenant people of God and the light symbolizes the covenant people as the light of the world. The angel previously explained that "these seven pipes are the eyes of the Lord, with an overview that encompasses the entire world." So, the seven lamp stands are called the eyes of the Lord, which symbolize that God's people will be like shining eyes.

These words were a great encouragement to the people of Israel, who had just been released from long captivity. These people had nothing of worth, nothing they could be proud of; nothing that other people could look up to them and respect them. The "self-portrait" of the Israelites resembled a broken mirror. There were many sorrows from the past, such miserable memories that they could never erase them from their minds, just as you cannot piece together a cracked mirror. It was very difficult for the Israelites to release the past and to feel encouraged that there would be a positive present and a fruitful future. They were like the disciples of Jesus who struggled to move their ship against a tremendous storm. Do you remember the story? Christ's disciples toiled all night and did all their best to "drive" their ship. When Christ appeared, they were terrified and said, "It is a ghost!" They could not believe that Jesus was real and that He would release them from their frightened situation. Thankfully the Lord released the disciples from their difficult situation. It happened to Zechariah as well. The Lord showed the vision to Zechariah to inspire him and to add the revelation: "Israel, you are the light of the world." Through your lamp stand and its light, your people will find truth, hope and life.

We Christians are also the light of the world. No matter how you perceive yourself or how others perceive you, by the grace of God, we, Christians are the light of the world. Isaiah 60:1-3 said, "Arise, shine, for your light has come and the glory of the Lord rises upon you. See, darkness covers the earth and thick darkness is over the people, but the Lord rises upon you and his glory appears over you. Nations will come to your light and kings to the brightness of your dawn." Christ also said to us, "You are the light of the world. A city on a hill cannot be hidden; neither do people light a lamp and put it under a bowl. Instead they put it on its stand, and by it gives light to everyone in the house. In the same way, let your light shine before man."(Matthew 5:14-16)

To make the lamp stand light up, oil should be supplied continuously. As I described before, the lamp stand that the Lord showed to the prophet had its own source of oil, which were the two olive trees. So, there never was a time when this lamp stand would lose its light. Within the Christian character that Jesus presented to us in the beatitudes: the mild heart, the merciful heart, the peacemaker's heart can be the light of the world. The person of purity, and humbleness and the person who thirsts for righteousness - can be the light of the world. In our human nature alone, we do not possess those qualities. But, when the Spirit of God supplies the oil, and makes our light burn, we can become the light of the world.

How do we shine to the world when we are in trials? We can find the wisdom in the word of Zechariah.

First, look up to God and have a dream.

The Lord wanted the prophet Zechariah to deliver the word of God to Zerubbabel, who was the leader of Israel at that time. Zerubbabel was weighed down by many burdens, because it was his task to restore the country that had been devastated, socially and spiritually. Just as there was huge mountain in the dream of the prophet, there was a huge obstacle for the Zerubbabel. Zerubbabel toiled hard, did all his best, but the mountain was so enormous to him that he despaired. To him the Lord said through the prophet Zechariah, "Who are you, O Great Mountain?" The Lord continued to say, "Before Zerubbabel, you shall become a plain! And, he shall bring forth the capstone with shouts of "Grace, grace to you"

Second, rely on the Spirit of God who would give us strength.

The Lord told Zechariah, "Not by might nor by power, but by My Spirit". That means that he would save his country not by his strength, but by the Spirit of God. It echoes in Paul's confession, "I can do everything through God who gives me strength". (Philippians 4:13)

Look up to God, Who Disciplines and Refines You Like Gold in Times of Suffering
1 Peter 5:5–7, Hebrews 12:5–13, Job 23:10

Hebrews 12:5–6 says that God expresses His love toward us by discipline: "And you have forgotten that word of encouragement that addresses as sons: 'My son, do not make light of the Lord's discipline, and do not lose heart when he rebukes you, because the Lord disciplines those he loves, and he punishes everyone he accepts as a son.'"

Let me first tell you what this Scripture does not mean. God's original intent is not to cause His children to suffer. Instead of suffering and pain, He wants to protect His children from any harm and bless them in many ways. God wants to give good lives to His children. God's plan for our lives is not to destroy us but to give us great futures with prosperity and abundant life: "'For I know the plans I have for you,' declares the Lord, 'plans to prosper you and not to harm you, plans to give you hope and a future'" (Jeremiah 29:10–11).

However, there will be occasions when we can not avoid suffering; God will allow it. The world we live now is not a perfect place; the Devil still plays a big part in this world's operation. Even Jesus said that we would suffer tribulations.

First of all, suffering promotes us to become mature and builds up our characters.

Paul said to the Romans, "And we boast in the hope of the glory of God. Not only so, but we also glory in our sufferings, because we know that suffering produces perseverance; perseverance, character; and character, hope. And hope does not put us to shame, because God's love has been poured out into our hearts through the Holy Spirit, who has been given to us" (Romans 5:2b–5, emphasis added). Our character is the "harvest of righteousness and peace" mentioned in Hebrews 12:11: "No discipline seems pleasant at the time, but painful. Later on, however, it produces a harvest of righteousness and peace for those who have been trained by it."

Suffering is not pleasant; rather, it is painful. However, it produces a harvest, forms a mature and understanding character, and refines us. That is our hope in times of suffering.

As I watched the Olympic athletes' performances, I was amazed by their beautiful artistry. It was amazing, but it was just the tip of the iceberg of their hard training, which required a lot of sweat and continuous effort. It was the result of their pain. Their beautiful performances are the harvest of the suffering. The winter 2009 Olympic figure skating gold medalist, Kim Yu Na, performed amazingly—artistic and beautifully. Not many people knew that she and her parents spent many tearful years of training to reach that level. As Job said, after trials, we "come forth as gold" (Job 23:10).

No pain, no gain!

No trials, no noble characters!

The great men and women in the Bible and in human history prove that character counts. David, Job, Joseph, Daniel, Moses, Abraham Lincoln, and countless other great people of history have proven this truth. Therefore, when you are discouraged in times of suffering and trials, look to the future with the hope that you will come out as refined gold. Rejoice in times of suffering by looking forward to the moment when you will stand at the podium to get God's gold medal.

God approves and loves those who overcome adversity and trials and become successful.

God will form you as a humble servant leader through suffering.

God wants His servants to become humble. Suffering and trials form you to become humble. That is what Peter says in 1 Peter 5:5–7: "Young men, in the same way be submissive to those who are older. All of you, clothe yourselves with humility toward one another, because God opposes the proud, but gives grace to the humble. Humble yourselves, therefore under God's mighty hand, that he may lift you up in due time. Cast away your anxiety on him because he cares for you."

Moses and David are good examples of those who became humble servants because of the discipline and trials they went through.

Moses, when he was young adult, was a patriot and had zeal for justice, yet he was never described as humble.

Moses' humbleness reached all over the face of the earth when he led the Israelites. Humbleness became his nature later; it flowed out of him from his everyday life naturally in his leadership. It was who he was. It took several decades for him to become a humble leader. There is an oriental saying: "When a decade passes, even the nature of the mountain and the river will change." That is required; no genius forms overnight. God spends a long time forming one person's character. I sometimes wonder why God is not so quick to use His servants; I have asked, "Why wait so long? Why does God waste His time and a person's life?" Because He knows that character counts: one leader can change the course of history and affect the lives of so many people.

Moses was in a high and noble position, the prince who could become the next king of Egypt, which was the strongest country of those days. He was highly trained and educated, and he was a strong man. He did not realize that he was arrogant and naughty then. God cast him out to the wilderness and had him spend forty years of his life as a shepherd in a foreign country. He spent his lonely and hard life there. His agony living in a foreign country was well expressed when he named his son Gershom, which means, "I have become an alien in a foreign land" (Exodus 2:22).

Saul's is another story of one who spent his painful life to harvest a humble character. God first chose Saul as a leader because he was a humble man, yet Saul became an arrogant king. God took him off the throne and chose David as the next king. David had the potential to become a humble man. God allowed him to experience trials and disciplined him so that he would form a character of humbleness. God anointed him when he was young, even before he fought and beat the giant, Goliath. Even after God had anointed him, it took a decade for him to become anointed as a real king at Hebron. After that, it still took eight more years for him to become the king of Israel at Jerusalem. During those eight years, he lived a hard life in the mountain dungeon because Saul chased after him to kill him. During those trials, David expressed his agony, saying, "I am like a dead dog." He felt bad and depressed many times. However, God allowed him to suffer in order to refine and carve the diamond character of humility inside him. The proverb said, "Iron sharpens iron" (Proverbs 27:17). I remember the days of my twenties when I felt so much pain because God was molding me as a humble person.. People say the twenties are beautiful, yet not for me; there were miserable days of humiliation and trials. I also remember the days when I was young captain, a junior Chaplain in Brussels Europe; felt sharp pain when God molded me as his humble servant. However, I realize now that those sharp irons formed me into who I am now.

If you feel pity for yourself because of the suffering you face, look up to God, who gives you the opportunity to become a humble servant leader!

Second, suffering helps you become a more understanding person; as a result, you become a good comforter to those who go through the same kind of suffering.

King David had gone through so much suffering. His experiences of suffering and various trials made him able to become a man of understanding and a real comforter. Many who had experienced hardship in their lives were able to gather around David because he was not just a boss to them but a friend; he was a comforter who understood their pain. He was like a magnet that pulls and draws others. David put his experience of suffering as a big highlighted letter when he wrote his resume as a leader. Likewise, you can put your experience of suffering on your résumé and highlight it: "I went through it. Been there, done that, understand you."

Suffering is on Jesus' résumé, as it was in Hebrews 4:14–16, "Therefore, since we have a great high priest who has ascended into heavens, Jesus the Son of God, let us hold firmly to the faith we profess. For we do not have a high priest who is unable to empathize with our weaknesses, but we have one who has been tempted in every way, just as we are—yet he did not sin. Let us then approach God's throne of grace with confidence, so that we may receive mercy and find grace to help us in our time of need." Jesus is our real comforter and wounded healer because He went through trials and suffered. Isaiah 53:3, 5 says, "He was despised and rejected by mankind, a man of suffering, and familiar with pain. But he was pierced for our transgressions, he was crushed for our iniquities; the punishment that brought us peace was on him, and by his wounds we are healed."

When you experience great trials, you may want to ask, "Do you know what I am saying, and can you understand what I am going through?" Jesus will say, "My son, daughter, I've been there, I've been gone through same like you," and He will put His arm around you and say, "I truly understand you; I am with you."

If you have a painful memory of your childhood or youth that you want to erase, you have two choices; one is to hold a grudge and be angry about the bad memories; another is to become a more understanding person. When you choose to become positive, your painful experience will help you become a good counselor and comforter to those who go through the same trouble that you experienced. Joyce Myer shared the experience of her painful childhood. She said that she became a real comforter and minister to those in trouble because she had gone through similar suffering. She said, "I know exactly what you are going through now, and God will understand you truly and will comfort you."1 (author's paraphrase)

Paul said in the 2 Corinthians 1:3–7,

Praise be to the God and Father of our Lord Jesus Christ, the Father of compassion and the God of all comfort, who comforts us in all our troubles, so that we can comfort those in any trouble with the comfort we ourselves receive from God. For just as we share abundantly in the sufferings of Christ, so also our comfort abounds through Christ. If we are distressed, it is for your comfort and salvation; if we are comforted, it is for your comfort, which produces in you patient endurance of the same sufferings we suffer. And our hope for you is firm, because we know that just as you share in our sufferings, so also you share in our comfort.

Jesus weeps with you when your spirit mourns. It was the same with Paul when he wrote the letter to the Corinthians (2 Corinthians 1:3–7).

If you are weary with the burden of life, do not fall into self-pity or complain. Look up to God, who refines your character into humbleness. It is the opportunity that God refines you like a pure diamond. Look at this as an opportunity for God to form you into a more understanding person who could become a real comforter for others.

Blessed are those who overcome difficulties and become real victors, who possess the humble, servant leader's character and who could comfort others. God will approve of those people's lives as the lives of real victors. God will be sure that they live blessed and beautiful lives.

Live a life of victor when life seems unfair
1 Samuel 24: 1-22

Do you sometimes feel that you want to get even? Listen to Paul's wisdom, "Leave room for God's wrath-- Let the justice of God take care of the case. If you love those who persecute you, you are actually heaping burning coals on his head." Here is the key word, "Do not be overcome by evil, but overcome evil with good." This is the best way. Keep your mind peaceful and protect the castle of your mind. New way of living a victorious life in time of unfair, injustice is to love the enemies and overcome the evil with kindness.

Today's scripture is 1st Samuel chapter 24. In this chapter, we can learn from David what it means to be man of a gentle heart. Although he was wrongly persecuted, he was seeking love and not revenge and practiced great love in this chapter. It is hard to be a world conqueror. Few people in history recognized as great conquerors, perhaps Alexander, the Great and Napoleon, etc. However, more less people have been able to conquer their mind because conquering the mind is harder than conquering the world. The proverb said, 'Conquering the mind is better than conquering the twelve castles.' The greatness of David is not his conquest of the world, but the conquest of his mind and the control of his anger when life seemed unfair.

In this chapter, we can learn from David what it means to be man of a gentle heart. Although he was wrongly persecuted, he was seeking love and not revenge and practiced great love in this chapter. It is hard to be a world conqueror. Few people in history recognized as great conquerors, perhaps Alexander, the Great and Napoleon, etc. However, more less people have been able to conquer their mind because conquering the mind is harder than conquering the world. The proverb said, 'Conquering the mind is better than conquering the twelve castles.' The greatness of David is not his conquest of the world, but the conquest of his mind and the control of his anger when life seemed unfair.

BOOK 5: NEW LIFE

Most of the story in this chapter deals with the portion of David's life as a man of suffering. It was the period when God disciplined him prior to his ascending to kingship. In this chapter, he did not resemble a strong leader nor a tough youth, but rather, a timid boy. Most people remember David as a great military leader, a fine warrior and a successful king. Others remember him as a poet or as a musician. Mostly, people remember David as a strong man. But not many people remember him as a 'generous and tender-hearted' man who in appearance resembled a timid boy. Although David had rough days, his tenderhearted character as a man whose heart followed the Lord was shown in this tough period.

As you know, Saul was jealous to David because David was more popular than him. He also was rising as Saul's political strong rival. He thought that David would possibly take his place. So, Saul hated David and plotted to get rid of him.

Saul attempted to assassinate young David on many occasions. One day when David played the harp for Saul, Saul suddenly threw a sword to kill him. This same incident happened many times. David realized that he was no longer safe in Saul's domain. David escaped to a mountain cave to run away from Saul's wrath. I am sure that David wanted to seek revenge against Saul because he unreasonably persecuted David. As a human he should had felt a strong desire to avenge Saul, who always looked for ways to end David's life. I am sure we all experience this feeling of revenge however insignificant. If they couldn't control their raged feeing, they could end up destroying others life and theirs as well.

The story of Hamlet is one of those instances. Anger can destroy others and it can swallow up our lives as well. I have seen many events that make life miserable because people could not control their anger and their feeling of revenge.

While you listening this story, try to position yourself in David's place to understand the situations of David's, because we also need to learn how to deal with unfair situation.

Now, let us look at the story of David. Since you know basic elements of the story, I do not have to re-tell the entire story. But, as a reminder, David became a hero after he was victorious in the battle with Goliath. The king at that time was Saul, who also was a great warrior. Both David and Saul were great warriors. Both Saul and David had excellent skills as warriors. Saul was excellent in throwing the sword. David threw the stone perfectly. Both worked hard to protect their tribe. There are other similarities between the two men. Both were country boys who became kings. They were not from the upper class. By contrast, however, one was political, the other' heart was tuned with God's heart.

King Saul felt insecure because people dearly loved the young, rising hero, David. Saul was also jealous of David. So, he attempted to assassinate David many times. Because of that, David had really difficult days and now he found himself hiding in a mountain cave. David even sighed, 'I am like a dog chased by many wolves.' David soothed himself by composing many poems, which are called Psalms. In those trying times, he wrote most of psalms, which were his prayer to God.

Listen what happened when Saul was looking for David's life. Just before David fled to the mountain caves, Saul was engaged in a severe war with the Philistines. Saul's army was pursuing the Philistines. When Saul returned, he received the report that, 'David was in the wilderness of Engedi.' Saul immediately responded and commanded his troop to capture David. "Let us go and get him." Saul's envy for his rival made him blind and he lost his sense of priority. He should have continued pursuing the Philistines because he did not finish the war with them. But instead, he called three thousand of his excellent soldiers to kill his rival, David. On the way, they reached to the place name, Engeldi.

Engeldi, where David hid, was the kind of natural refuge because there were lots of caves. Outcasts from society could safely hide themselves at Engeldi. The location of Engeldi means, "The rocks of the wild goats". It symbolized that David had a wild life in the mountains and caves.

King Saul had a natural calling emergency on the way to overtake David. Verse 3 illustrates that Saul had to cover his feet. It was a very funny story and a very natural one. I will not go into detail, but if you are curious, ask me later on. The cave was a very good hiding place and King Saul needed to hide his feet in the cave. It was a dark and had a safe enclosure. But Saul did not realize that David and his followers were in the back of the same cave. While King Saul was still caring for his feet, David's followers found that the persecutor of their master, who had just come to kill David, was right there before them completely defenseless. One shot could kill Saul and took away David's enemy. The man said to David, "This is the day the Lord spoke of when He said to you, 'I will give your enemy into your hands for you to deal with as you wish.' He was saying that it was David's God-given chance to get rid of the enemy, Saul. What do you think you would have done, if you were in that situation? What did David do? He crept up to Saul very quietly and cut off a corner of Saul's robe. David refused to take this excellent opportunity for revenge; instead David spared the life of his enemy. David went out of the cave and called Saul loudly, "My Lord, when the Lord delivered me into your hands and someone urged me to harm you, but I spared your life. See, my father, look at this piece of your robe in my hand."

Why didn't David kill his enemy? There were two reasons.

First if all, it was because Saul was an anointed servant of God. David was conscience-stricken for even having cut off a corner of the robe of God's anointed one. We see here David had reverence for God and his reverence for God forbade him from taking the life of God's anointed one. As a matter of fact, God gives all life and therefore God anoints all human beings, even though there are some different degrees of anointment. So, reverence of life comes from reverence of God.

Second, David believed that God would be a fair judge; He also believed that God would bring justice between Saul and himself. Listen to what he said, "I have not wronged you, but you are hunting me down to take my life. May the Lord judge between you and me. And may the Lord avenge the wrongs you have done to me, but my hand will not touch you. As the old saying goes, 'From evildoers come evil deeds,' so my hand will not touch you. May the Lord be our judge and decide between us." David gave up all of his anger and feeling of betrayal and any desire to seek retribution. He gave those to the Lord. He could do that because he believed that, God definitely would be fair even though people were not fair. David trusted God's justice would win even though humans were unfair.

Let me quote the wise advice of Paul. "Bless those who persecute you. Bless, not curse. Remember, render to no man, evil for evil; Do not repay anyone evil for evil. Do not seek revenge, my friends, but leave room for God's wrath, for it is written, 'It is Mine to avenge'. I will repay, says the Lord. On the contrary, 'If your enemy is hungry, feed him; if he is thirsty, give him something to drink. In doing this, you will heap burning coals on his head. Do not overcome by evil, but overcome evil with good. " (Romans 12: 14-21)

Loving our enemy is the highest value of Christian. It is also the wisdom whereby we deal with feelings of revenge. We also can learn "How to win! Who is the winner?"

What is the best way to handle someone who has wronged you? What is the wisest way to deal with the situation when you find yourself in an unjust situation?

Let me conclude today's sermon with the Christ's Sermon on the Mount. "You have heard that it hath been said, "An eye for an eye, and a tooth for a tooth. But, I say to you, that you resist not an evil person. But whoever smites you on the right cheek, turn to him the other also. Whoever compels you to go a mile, go with him two miles" Remember, 2000 years ago, God's appointed one, Jesus Christ, went more than two miles for us and He walked far to the cross and even gave up His life for us. Love your enemy; do not try to get even, because God's justice will make it all even. Be not controlled by evil, but overcome evil with good.

Live a life of victor when Life seems too tough
Job 1:1–22, John 9:1–12

Can you keep on trusting God when bad things happen around you, when the pain is sharp and the doubt is deep and it is impossible to see the sense in it all? Yes, we can continue trusting God if we look at things in His perspective.

Life is a continuing response to challenges. The challenges in our lives will be over when our lives end. Some people will fall because they cannot overcome their challenges. However, those who overcome and win their trials will become much stronger and mature people. How you look at a problem determines how you will get through it. The positive perspective that God gives will help you overcome your problems and become victorious. You may start with the same situation as someone else, but the result will be totally different if you look at the problem with God's positive perspective and someone else doesn't.

When someone suffers, what is the response of those who know that suffering is the consequences of sin? They immediately think that something happened to the person because of the person's sin. However, bad things can happen to the good people.

The lives of Job and Joseph in the ancient days teach us about the problem of evil. Jesus also answered to this problem profoundly when His disciples asked, to paraphrase John 9:2, "How was this man born blind? What did he or his parents do wrong?" He defended the man who was born blind: "Neither this man nor his parents sinned,' said Jesus, 'but this happened so that the works of God might be displayed in him'" (John 9:3).

I first want to talk about Job's life to suggest a new perspective on suffering. God defended Job and said He was upright, yet God allowed Satan to attack Job temporarily.

Job lived around 2000 BC and experienced tremendous suffering. He was overwhelmed with sorrow and pain. He was anguished over the burden and hardship of life. His suffering was unbearable, and his pain was beyond his capacity to absorb. Job was afflicted with sores from the bottom of his feet to the top of his head. He took a piece of broken pottery and tried to scrape the sores away. This trial was only a small part of his sufferings. The orthodox theology of that period said that if someone suffers or experiences a disaster, it is because of her sin. God is bringing judgment upon her.

However, this prevailing philosophy is reversed in the book of Job! Throughout the book, our Lord demonstrates a very important truth that not all human suffering is caused by sin.

The book of Job clearly says that Job was upright with the Lord and was blameless and shunned evil. In Job chapter one, there is an interesting conversation between God and Satan that illustrates the purity of Job's soul: "Then the Lord said to Satan, 'Have you considered my servant, Job? There is no one on earth like him; he is blameless and upright, a man who fears God and shuns evil. And he still maintains his integrity, though you incited me against him to ruin him without any reason" (Job 2:3, emphasis added). The Lord said clearly that Job's suffering was given to him not because of his sin but because Satan caused him to suffer. God allowed him to go through trials, but the bottom line is that Job's suffering was not caused by sin. This inspired book radically changed the prevailing theology. It laid the profound theology that even good people could suffer.

Job was the wealthiest, happiest, and most blessed person in the East. God was very proud of Job because of his integrity. Job also was the richest man in those days. In Job Chapter 1 verse 2, it said that "he had 3,000 camels" and that was only one portion of his possessions. In the desert, a camel was very important as it was the best form of transportation. If we compare a camel with a contemporary means of transportation, a camel would be like a Cadillac or a Mercedes-Benz. So, he had 3,000 Benzes, and that was only a part of his possessions.

Trials started to come to Job. Let me refresh your memory with what Job had to endure. Job 1:13–15 reads, "One day when Job's sons and daughters were feasting and drinking wine at the oldest brother's house, a messenger came to Job and said, 'the oxen were plowing and the donkeys were grazing nearby, and the Sabeans attacked and carried them off. They put the servants to the sword, and I am the only one who has escaped to tell you!'"

Job 1:16 reads, "A few seconds later, more bad news came, 'The fire of God fell from the sky and burned up the sheep and the servants, and I am the only one who has escaped to tell you!'"

Job 1:17 reads, "Another messenger came and said, 'The Caldeans formed three raiding parties and swept down on your camels and carried them off. They put the servants to the sword, and I am the only one who has escaped to tell you!'"

Job 1:18 reads, "While he was still speaking, yet another messenger came and said, 'Your sons and daughters were feasting and drinking wine at the oldest brother's house, when suddenly a mighty wind swept in from the desert and struck the four corners of the house. It collapsed on them and they are dead.'"

Finally, all was gone: his family, his possessions, and his health. All that was left was severe suffering.

Natural catastrophe, war, and terror smashed Job's life, and he managed all of those losses. However, when the tragedy came to his loving children, he became angry and expressed his unbearable pain. He tore his robe and shaved his head.

What would you say if you were in that situation? Job immediately fell to the ground and said, "Naked I came from my mother's womb, and naked I will depart. The Lord gave and the Lord has taken away; may the name of the Lord be praised" (Job 1:21).

Still more afflictions befell Job. "Satan went out and inflicted Job with painful sores" (Job 2:7). Job's wife said to him, "Are you still holding on to your integrity? Curse God and die!" (Job 2:9). But Job's response was still a song of loyalty to God: "You are talking like a foolish woman. Shall we accept good from God, and not trouble?"

While sitting on ashes, his head was shaved and his robe was torn. His friends were unable to recognize him. It was an unspeakable moment. Although not many people goes through extreme misery like Job, but we go through similar kinds of problems once in a while in our lives. What would you say about these problems? What perspective would your friends give if you faced these problems?

In Job's situation, his friends came to give their counsel. One of his closest friends, Eliphaz, said, "Job, my good friend, I want to say something to you. I know you are experiencing great stress. I feel pity for you. But I have to tell you this: you are suffering because you have done something wrong" (author's interpretation of Job 4:7–9 and Job chapter 12). Scripture tells that Eliphaz says, "Consider, now: Who, being innocent, has ever perished? Where were the upright ever destroyed? As I have observed, those who plow evil and those who sow trouble reap it. At the breath of God they perish; at the blast of his anger they are no more" (Job 4:7–9). Isn't it cruel to say that? He is not really helping his friend. He is only adding pain to Job's heart.

Now, another close friend of Job's said, "Dominion and awe belong to God; he establishes order in the heights of heaven. Can His forces be numbered? Upon whom does his light not rise? How then can a mortal be righteous before God? How can one born of woman be pure? If even the moon is not bright, and the stars are not pure in his eyes, how much less a mortal, who is but a maggot—a human being, who is only a worm!" (Job 25:2–6).

I think Job's friends wanted to help Job, and their motivation was neither to irritate nor to discourage him. Their advice and wisdom were out of genuine friendship and love. If you look at Job 2:11–13, you will find that genuine love displayed. "They set out from their homes and met together by agreement to go and sympathize with him and comfort him. When they saw him from a distance, they could hardly recognize him; they began to weep aloud, and they tore their robes and sprinkled dust on their heads. Then they sat on the ground with him for seven days and seven nights. During those seven days and seven nights, no one said a word to him, because they saw how great his suffering was."

Their advice and comfort looked so wise and godly. However, it added more pain to Job than the suffering itself. What was the problem? They gave the wrong perspective to this poor suffering man. They applied the wrong theology to this blameless person. They were like physicians who gave the wrong medicine to their patients.

Let's say that there is excellent pain medicine, such as morphine. Morphine works wonderfully well to stop pain. However, if the doctor prescribes morphine to the wrong person, this great medicine would become harmful. Likewise, Job's friend applied the wrong spiritual medicine. His wrong perspective worsened Job's sorrow, and Job became furious. "You smear me with lies; you are worthless physicians, all of you! If only you would be altogether silent! For you that would be wisdom" (Job 13:4–5). They gave Job a negative perspective because they had a misconception about the problem of evil. Sadly, that is what many believers do to their loved ones: penalize, condemn, and put guilt on their loved ones' burned hearts.

However, throughout the book of Job, our Lord demonstrates a very important truth: not all human suffering is caused by sin. Jesus Christ's profound answer to the problem of evil echoes with the theology of Job:

One day, while Jesus was walking on the street in Judea, He saw a man born blind from birth. Here is a paraphrase of the scene: His disciples started to ask, "Why did this tragedy happen to this poor man?" They felt very sorry for the blind man. They wondered, "Why are there always people who have to suffer in this world? Is it because God does not love them, or does God have limited power? Perhaps God just does not care." The disciples arrived to their own conclusion according to the traditional teaching and asked their teacher, Jesus: "Rabbi, who sinned, this man or his parents, that he was born blind?" Their view about the tragedy was exactly like the one that Job's friends held. They firmly believed that when someone experienced pain, it was God's punishment for someone's sin. The rabbis had developed the principle that "there is no death without sin, and there is no suffering without iniquity." They were even capable of thinking that a child could sin in the womb or that its soul might have sinned in a preexistent state. Rabbis also maintained the theory that terrible punishment came to certain people because of their parents' sins.

Let us pause to review their thoughts. Is it really possible that a baby in a mother's womb could commit sin? Is it possible that someone could sin even before he visibly existed and was born into the world?

Although human beings are born with Adam's original sin, children not yet exposed to the temptation of sin are innocent. It is not logical that someone can sin before she is born into the world. Was this man born blind because of his parents' sins? That would not be fair for him. Contrary to the old beliefs, our Lord Jesus adamantly answered His disciples that neither this man nor his parents sinned! It was a simple and short proclamation. However, it was a radical statement in those days. It also was a final word of highest judge.

What a great relief to hear what Jesus said. Nothing is wrong! Jesus explained that the man was born blind so that the work of God might be displayed. Jesus proclaimed that He was the light of the world. To paraphrase, "I'm the light of the world. As long as it is day, I must do the work of God who sent Me. Night is coming, when no one can work." Jesus had seen this poor man's life through God's perspective. He believed that God had something to do with this man being born blind.

Jesus looked at this man's life positively because He knew that his life was in God's hands.

Jesus looked at the blind man's trial in the light of God.

Jesus believed that God had a purpose for this man and that it was not an accident for him to be born blind.

I am sure that the man who was born blind heard Jesus said positively about his blindness. No doubt he had an overwhelming thought, such as Wahoo! God's glory and His mighty work will be displayed through me. Since the man who was born blind accepted Jesus' positive thought, he took the method of Jesus' healing very positively. He did not complain when Jesus put dirt on his eye, and he obeyed when Jesus told him to wash his eye at the pool of Siloam to receive sight.

Let us learn Jesus' positive perspective.

When something goes wrong, our immediate thought is to find someone to blame or to blame ourselves: "What did I do wrong? What did you do wrong?" It could be true sometimes that we did do something wrong and got the result of it. However, even in those cases, God has a plan to make things better and display His wisdom and mighty work and love.

Another of the Old Testament stories that echoes Jesus' positive perspective is that of Joseph. When he was in his teens, his brothers sold him to foreigners as a slave. Well, at one point Joseph was imprisoned, having been caught in a conspiracy and wrongly accused of raping the wife of his lord. Joseph sometimes was starved and suffered great loneliness. He went through lots of suffering. He experienced hardship that wasn't his fault. He was an upright man like Job. If he had looked at his life in a negative way, he would have killed himself or become an angry man bent on revenge.

However, he looked at his life according to the providential will of God and trusted the Lord in every situation. Later on, God blessed Joseph and made him the prime minister of Egypt, which was the strongest nation in those days. He expressed his belief when he was reunited with his brothers. Joseph said to them, "You intended to harm me, but God intended it for good to accomplish what is now being done, the saving of many lives" (Genesis 50:19).

Suffering sometimes could be the consequence of misconduct and sin. However, it is not always the case. Misfortune is not necessarily based on one's sinfulness. As a matter of fact, there are many cases when suffering visits good people. That was especially true in Job's case. Feelings of guilt come when we face trials and troubles in life. However, no longer must we dwell on our guilt because we misunderstand the cause of our suffering. We have to remember that good people also can suffer. Job never lost his sense of hope, although he faced tremendous suffering and was in a seemingly hopeless situation. This was because he believed in the providential will of God and trusted the Lord completely. Job said, "God understands the way to it and he alone knows where it dwells, for he views the ends of the earth and sees everything under the heavens" (Job 28:23–24). God has a purpose for us when we face life's hardships, even though we often do not understand why we are being scourged. However, God does understand, because God knows all things and views the end of suffering. Job said a famous phrase when he was in a great suffering: "After all the trials, I will come forth as gold" (Job 23:10). Taking on God's positive perspective will enable one to be a highly effective person who achieves the highest goals in spite of life's trials.

Job, Joseph, and the man who was born blind and received sight became accomplished people like gold medalists in the Olympics; they glorified God through their trials

Now, allow me to quote words about attitude from Dr. Norman Vincent Peal on his book, "The Power of Positive Thinking": "Do this with an attitude of faith and you will receive sufficient strength and ability to deal with this problem. Later, if you wish, we can go into analysis of your basic problem."[2]

Harold S. Kushner, Rabbi emeritus, wrote the forward message in the book of Viktor E. Frankl, Man's Searching for Meaning: "Forces beyond your control can take away everything you possess except one thing, your freedom to choose how you will respond to the situation.

You cannot control what happens to you in life, but you can always control what you will feel and do about what happens to you." 3

We can either choose to become morose, staggered by the weight of the trial and consider the bitter taste of that trial like the sour taste of a lemon or we can choose to deal with that trial with a positive attitude and make that lemon into lemonade.

People who are in bad heath, having financial difficulties, or struggling in their marriages lose hope not just because of their difficult situations but because they think negatively. As believers and followers of Christ, we should think like Christ and be positive in any situation. We should look at our lives in the light of God's good providential will.

At this time, I want to encourage you to look at the problems you and others face with God's positive perspective. I've seen so many people's lives become more miserable and hurt not because of what they had faced but because of their friends' negative comments and, most of all, their negative perspective on their lives. Get a new perspective through Jesus. Believe in God's love and His good will for your life. Develop a deep faith in God that will give you faith in yourself. I pray for you to look at God, who is the ultimate good, who would bring good even out of evil. Keep on trusting God even through hardship. May God give you a positive perspective, bless you, and shine upon your life, that you would become happy and victorious even in times of trouble.

Privileges of New life

All of the youth group kids who came back from mission trip to Czechoslovakia said one thing in unison about their experiences, "We will never complain about living in my country. It is such a blessing to live in this country." One of the advantages of sending our children on mission trip is that they would recognize thoroughly that they are living in the most blessed country. Yes, it is such a blessing to be a United States citizen; we have religious freedom, lots of opportunities and material blessings. Being Children of God will be even more of a blessing as Jesus said, "I am the vine and you are the branches. If a man remains in Me, and I remain in him, he will bear much fruit." Jesus promised that life in Him should be an abundant life. Do you enjoy the abundance of life that is available to you by dwelling in Christ? Do you really enjoy the blessedness of being a Christian?

In this chapter, I am going to talk specifically what are the privileges of having a new life in Christ Jesus.

1. We will experience miracles in our life

2. We will have a privilege to call God as ABBA FATHER

3. We will have real joy and happiness

4. We will live bold and courageous life

5. We will inherit God's kingdom

We will experience miracles in our life: God's Almighty Power Makes Miracles Still Possible Isaiah 38:1–8

Miracles happen not just through the great prophets like Elijah, but also through common people just like you and me and through our honest prayer. The unseen Hand of God is always with us. Just reach out to Him. It is our, who have a new life, privilege to reach to the hand of God who would protect, save, preserve, and met our needs with His miracles. Therefore, all we need do is to open our eyes and our hearts to the true possibility of miracles and depend on God's love. God wants to provide all that we need through His Providence. Because our God is a living God, He still performs miracles. James 5:16-18 speaks that common prayers of believers would bring miracles and it reads, "The prayer of a righteous man is powerful and effective. Elijah was a man just like us. He prayed earnestly that it would not rain, and it did not rain on the land for three and one half years. Again he prayed and the heavens gave rain, and the earth produced its crops."

Hezekiah was going to die soon. He prayed God hard to give him more life. The Lord gave him 15 more years to live. As a sign for that the Lord made the sunlight step back ten steps. How could this happen? It was the miracles of God. Miracles impinge upon Christianity.

I want to tell you an awesome story from Isaiah 38:1–8. When King Hezekiah heard that he was going to die soon, he prayed to God desperately and asked Him to give him life. The Lord heard and answered his prayer, giving him fifteen more years to live. As a sign, the Lord made the sunlight step back ten steps.

Let me tell you one more story from the Old Testament, Joshua 10:12–14. Joshua and the entire Israelites' army marched all night to engage in war with Israel's enemies. Probably at dawn, they used a surprise tactic to attack the enemies. The Israelites' army was victorious, and the enemy, the Amorites, ran away. The Israelites chased them, but the sun was going down. Joshua then said to the Lord in the presence of Israel, "O sun, stand still over Gideon. O moon, stand over the valley of Aijalon." So, the sun stood still and the moon stopped until the nation of Israel avenged its enemies. In the historical record, the Book of Jashar, it was written, 'The sun stopped in the middle of the sky and delayed going down about a full day. There has never been a day like it before or since, a day when the Lord listened to a man.' " (Joshua 10:12–14)

Let us ponder for a minute to see how these phenomena happened. The sun rises in the east and moves toward the west, and this is always true, no matter where you live, because the Earth orbits the sun clockwise. This is a natural phenomenon that God arranged to make it possible for human beings to live stable lives according to an unchangeable time frame. It is a good thing that God created the concept of time to allow us to live according to a rhythm; variety and expectancy mysteriously work together in this time frame. Genesis 8:22 reads, "As long as the earth endures, seedtime and harvest, cold and heat, summer and winter, day and night will never cease." Time is the basic and essential fabric of every living creature's life span. As the sun continues to move from east to west, time passes and years go into the future; the future becomes the present as we age. Eventually, all of us will reach the end of our time, the end of our lives. Our time is in His hands, as Psalm 31:15a and 24 say: "My times are in your hands ... be strong and take heart, all you who hope in the Lord."

Dr. Paul Tournier, a Swiss doctor, has a book called The Seasons of Life, in which he writes, "Sickness can suddenly overtake us at the very height of career and in the full frenzy of activity, with the same blow breaking it and, in some way, revealing it emptiness. Then it is that a man needs to find someone with whom he can talk about the problems besieging his mind."[1]

Each of our lives has its seasons, which may be compared to the seasons of the year. There is childhood—springtime; youth and young adulthood—exuberant summer season; the autumn of maturity and the winter of aging. Each of us is born into the world with the expectation of spending the whole year here and experiencing all its seasons. But some live only through the springtime, some enjoy the excitement of summer, some get to see the turning of the leaves in the mellow time; still others stay until the snow blankets the ground.

Hezekiah wanted to experience all the seasons of life, yet he didn't get the privilege to live a full life span. He had done great things for his country with his faith and his loving heart. He had experienced the season of blossoming; he overcame the hardships of life and had successes, and he became a famous and victorious king. Things were getting settled and stabilized. However, in his prime age, when he arrived at the time to enjoy peace after having passed through all his life's trials and storms, he faced death because of a severe disease.

All of a sudden, an unwelcome visitor knocked on his door: sickness and death. He cried out, "Now, Lord, you want me to be sick and die!" As you can see, Hezekiah was not just fearing death but also experiencing deep sorrow because he had to separate from his loved ones as you can read on Isaiah 38:11b, "No longer will I look on mankind, or be with those who now dwell in this world." Mankind and people who dwell with King Hezekiah were his loved ones and associates (author' interpretation)

He felt a terrible sense of loss; he thought he had earned happiness and lovely people through his life's hard work, yet sickness and death were going to rob him of all of that: "In the prime of my life must I go through the gates of death and be robbed of the rest of my years?" I said, "I will not again see the Lord, the Lord, in the land of the living; no longer will I look on mankind, or be with those who now dwell in this world … like a weaver I have rolled up my life, and he has cut me off from the loom; day and night you made an end of me. I cried a swift or thrush, I moaned like a morning dove. My eyes grew weak as I looked to the heavens. I am troubled; O Lord … For the grave cannot praise you, death cannot sing your praise; those who go down to the pit cannot hope for your faithfulness" (Isaiah 38:10–11, 18, emphasis added).

He felt helpless. He could not find any strength in himself or his friends or from his power as king of a nation that had just been victorious against Assyria, the strongest country on those days. Nothing could help him.

So, this is what happened next:

- Hezekiah desperately prayed to God.
- Hezekiah turned his face to the wall and prayed to the Lord. He wept bitterly, mourned like a dove, and cried like a swift or thrush (verse 14).
- The Lord answered his prayer; He saw his tears.
- Good news came to him; God's prophet, Isaiah, brought the message directly, "I have heard your prayer and seen your tears; I will add fifteen years to your life."
- A miracle happened. As the sunlight stepped back ten steps, God rearranged nature.

With the amazing miracle of sunlight stepping back ten steps, God pushed time back only for one person, Hezekiah. God pushed the sun back to give fifteen more years of life for only one person, Hezekiah. This event was more amazing than if the sun had just stayed in place, as it had with the order of Joshua. I want you to imagine standing before the sun like Hercules and pushing the sun with all your strength. Can you move it an inch? Can you move it 0.00001 millimeters? No, nothing can happen with your power. But God did, with His mighty power; He pushed the sun one, two … ten steps back!

Now, guess what I want to discuss with this story? The miracles of God! Miracles impinge upon Christianity, and they are possible because of God's almighty power. We cannot be believers of the Bible or be Christians if we do not believe in miracles, because the Bible contains many stories of miracles from Genesis to Revelation.

The major pillars of our faith are based on the miracles of God:

God's creation of the universe and human beings was a miracle.

The birth of Jesus Christ from the Virgin Mary was a miracle. Jesus' birth was not just difficult; it was impossible. Mary was a virgin. Only God could breathe life into her womb. And just as God caused her to conceive the perfect sinless Savior—fully God, fully human—He can accomplish, through you, those things that seem impossible in your life.

So much of God's redemptive history involves miracles that cannot be explained by human reason or natural law. The miracles prevail not only in the Old Testament but in the New Testament as well:

- ○ Jesus fed more than five thousand with only two fish and five loaves of bread.
- ○ Jesus Christ raised Lazarus from the dead.
- ○ Jesus healed the man who was born blind.
- ○ Most of all, He was raised from death and resurrected.

If we are not open to the possibility of miracles, we should delete many of the stories from the Bible. If we remove these stories, we deny the foundation of Christianity. Now, how do we define miracles? What is a miracle? Erickson's theology of "Miracle and Providence" gives answer to this question.

"Simply, it is a supernatural event, an unusual event that cannot be explained by common sense because it contradicts natural law. Water always should flow from up to down because of the law of gravity. When water goes up, it is a miracle. Let me tell you how miracles can occur. Miracles happen when supernatural forces counter natural forces. The laws of nature are not suspended; they continue to operate, but supernatural intervention negates their effects. Water can go up, even if the law of gravity continues to function, when the unseen hand of God is beneath the water. God simply could change the law of gravity, if it is His will.

If we are open to the possibility that there are realities and forces outside the system of nature, then why can't we believe that miracles are possible? Billy Graham said, "If we believe in the mighty power of God, why can't we believe—even if the Bible said that Jonah swallowed the whale!" 2 (author's paraphrase of Erickson' view on Miracle and God's Providence)

But our Christian view of a miracle goes a little further. A Miracle is a special supernatural work of God's providence that happens at the right time and at the right place to accomplish His divine purpose.

Erickson' view on the miracle is correct when he wrote, "Miracles happen when the people of God pray for help at the time of our need." 3 The importance of the miracle in Christianity is not whether it is supernatural or not, but it accomplishes God' sovereign will and provide His abound grace to us.

Durfee Martin wrote the hymnal, "Do not dismayed'. Betide" sang: 'Through days of toil when the heart doth fail, God will take care of you. When dangers fierce your path assail, God will take care of you. All you may need; He will provide; God will take care of you; nothing you ask will be denied. God will take care of you' (Durfee Martin, 1994 , emphasis added).

Since God still performs miracles, it is our conviction that we are in the hands of a good, wise, and powerful God who will accomplish His will at the right time and in the right place to glorify Himself and to meet our needs.

More importantly, trust that God will give you victory over the terrible power of death; God raised Jesus from the grave with His almighty power and conquered the power of death for Hezekiah.

Trust God, who is almighty and powerful! Live a powerful life with the strength God gives you!

For Reflection and Discussion

1. How does time control life? Discuss this in terms of the lives of King Hezekiah and Joshua (Isaiah 38:1–8, Joshua 10:12–14).

2. Think about the four seasons of life according to Dr. Paul Tournier's book, The Seasons of Life. What could you learn from Hezekiah's experience of deliverance from serious sickness and death, and what could you learn from his prayer?

3. What do you learn about God, who answered Hezekiah's prayer?

4. How did God give strength to the person who faced death and needed help desperately?

5. What is the miracle? What is the definition of a miracle in Christian faith?

6. Have you experienced a miracle in your life? Discuss it with your group. Give all attendees the opportunity to talk about their personal experiences with miracles.

We will have a privilege to call God as ABBA FATHER: Our Father in Heaven
Matthew 6: 5-15, Romans 8:15-17

Jesus said, "This is how you should pray, Our Father who art in Heaven, Hallowed Be Thy Name!" If we find out the how great privilege it is to call God as our Father, we would have abundant new life. I want to talk this more specifically. Roman chapter 8:15 said, "For you did not receive a spirit that makes you a slave again to fear, but you received the Spirit of son-ship. We can call God as "Abba, Father!" God is our Father and we are His children. The strong bond between parents and children is trust and love. Perfect love drives out all fear in a relationship. The Holy Spirit himself testified that we are God's children. What is the first thing that happened in the relationship between God and humankind when Adam and Eve disobeyed God? "They were afraid of God." They hid themselves from God and tried to get away from God. Once love is driven out of a relationship, fear sets in. The relationship was broken. However, now since we are united with God, the Creator, We can call God, the Father as 'Abba Father'! What a great privilege it is!

The word, Father or Mother, in all languages is very similar. In Hebrew father is "Abba", in English it is Father or Papa, in Korean, Appa; in Chinese, Bue or Papa; in French, Pere or Papa. I think the title of Father sounds almost the same from language to language because in all countries children have the same portrait and personal relationships with their fathers. If someone asked you right now 'Can you tell us about your father?', what would you say? I think everyone would have different things to say, yet everyone will have some basic common points.

Now, when Jesus taught His disciples how to pray, He first taught them to call God, the Person to whom you pray as, "Our Father in Heaven". Nowadays, when we pray, it is natural and very normal for us to pray to God as Our Heavenly Father. However, in the days of Jesus, this title that Jesus gave to God was a radical expression. On those old days, people thought that God was only a spiritual, fearful Supreme Being. So, humankind could never approach God with such an intimacy. God was always a Holy Being, far away from humans. When Jesus came, He taught the nearness of God to us; God's presence is as near as our Father to us. And the New Testament teaches us that we can even call our Father in heaven as "Abba" just as children call their father as "Papa" When we pray, calling God as "Abba, Father," there is trust , love , closeness , respect and honor. A father is one who takes care of us; who provides everything for our needs, nurtures and guides us.

Let us take a look at the Sermon on the Mount. A model for prayer is one part of the Sermon on the Mount. Christ taught His disciples to trust God's provision like children trusting their father's care. Christ said, "Look at the birds of the air; they do not sow or reap or store away in barns, and yet your heavenly Father feeds them. Are you much more valuable than they? " (Matthew 6: 26) Christ also said, "Do not worry 'what shall we wear' 'what shall we eat' because your Heavenly Father knows that you need them." (Matthew 6: 31-32) When you pray, pray to God as if He is your father! God is a perfect father, who already knows our needs. Like a good parent, God already recognizes our needs. He thinks ahead of us. Therefore, trust and believe God totally.

Remember that prayer is not just informing God about what we need, but instead, prayer is the attitude of totally trusting God as Our Father. Prayer includes petition, but it is far more than that. It is opening oneself to God with trust. Prayer opens the way of God's blessings that He already has stored for us in heaven.

Jesus also taught us to address God as, "Our Father" not as "My Father". Christ is not denying your personal relationship with God, but is simply teaching us that we are one congregation under His care. When we call God 'Our Father' in the close unit of the congregation or in the close unit of the family, we can comprehend God's intimacy with us, but when we call God 'Our Father' in a prayer of whole nations, the meaning of prayer is quite different.

Take this example. There was a championship soccer game, and two teams were in the final competition. One team's name was, "Hallelujah;" the other team's name was "Praise the Lord." Both teams prayed to God, "Father, give my team victory!" Team Hallelujah shot the ball into the goal. Team Hallelujah shouted, "Hallelujah." The Praise the Lord team shot the ball into the goal and shouted, "Praise the Lord " Back and forth, back and forth both teams would score goals, and then, shout out their particular praise. How many times we think that God is "only on our side". Both teams should remember that God is the Father of both teams, not just the Father of one particular side. Therefore, our prayer should always be completed with the prayer of "Thy Will be done." In regard of this concept, there was a true story came from the pages of the Civil War. Whenever General Lee of the Confederate Army prayed, he would pray for victory for his own army, but he ultimately prayed that the Lord's will be done.

Jesus also taught us to address God, As the Father In Heaven. It makes a balance of God's nearness with His transcendence, which means that God is above us. God is our Father, but He is not earthly Being nor is He secular. He is ever near, but is to be held in reverence. Although God is very approachable, He remains a transcendent God. Therefore, we have to approach Him with reverence and awe. And the first priority of our prayer should be, "Hallowed Be Thy Name." As His children, the beginning of our prayer should be a request to God that His name would be highly lofted. "Our Father who art in Heaven, Hallowed Be Thy Name." Name identifies the character of someone. It also reveals who they are. Likewise, God's character and the supreme qualities of His person are identified and revealed through His names. Therefore, we can understand God better through His names. More importantly, if we know the One to whom we pray, we can pray correctly. Every religion has some form of prayer, and the object for prayer. In fact, almost every human being prays. As Paul found in Athens, Greece, that some prayed to an "Unknown God". As Believers of Holy Scripture, we have to know the God to whom we pray. Our God reveals Himself through His Names. Scripture unveils twelve names of our God. I would like to introduce a few of His names.

First, Elohim (Almighty)

Elohim is the first name that we could find in the first chapter of Genesis. Elohim means God who is Almighty. It is used 2700 times in the original Hebrew text of the Bible as God's name. In the English Bible, God is identified as Elohim and translated as 'Almighty God' only 32 times. "In the Beginning, Ellohim created the heavens and the earth." (Genesis 1:1) "Elohim said, 'Let there be light' and there was light.' (Genesis1:3)" Elohim said, "Be fruitful, increase in number." (Genesis 1: 28) The Apostle Paul said in Romans 1: 20, "For the invisible things of him from the creation of world are clearly seen, being understood by the things that are made, even his eternal power." God, the Almighty asked the question to Job, "Where were you when I laid the earth's foundation? Tell me, if you can understand who marked off its dimensions? Surely you know! Who stretched a measure line across it? Can you bind the beautiful Pleiades? Can you loose the cords of Orion? Can you bring the constellations in their seasons? " (Job 38:3-31) In Job chapter 38, God's name was used as Elohim because the creator of the universe is the Almighty God. We pray to our Almighty God, Elohim, whose name we should glorify and hallow.

Second, El Shaddai

El means great and glorious. Shaddai means nourishment, satisfaction, or supply. So, El +Shaddai means "The One who is mighty to completely nourish, satisfy and supply us." God's name as El Shaddai appeared 48 times in the Old Testament. When Abraham was so depressed after a long journey, God appeared to him and said, Genesis 17:1, "I am Almighty God; walk before me and be blameless. I will confirm my covenant between you and Me and you will greatly increase your name." When God said, "I am Almighty" in Genesis 17:1, in Hebrew He was saying that, "EL Shaddai, Almighty One, who can supply and nourish you perfectly." So, when you pray to God in heaven, remember that He is the One who can nourish you and give you perfect satisfaction. As the Psalmist confessed, "The Lord indeed gives what is good and our land will yield its harvest." (Psalm 85:12)

Third, Jehovah

Another God's name is Jehovah which means "to Be". Jehovah, as one of the names of God, was the most commonly used title in the Old Testament. It was used as God's name approximately 6800 times. When God called Moses to free the Israelites from Egypt and Pharaoh, Moses was afraid that the Israelites would reject his leadership. So Moses asked God, "Suppose, I go to the Israelites and say to them, 'the God of your fathers has sent me to you to lead you and free you from the bondage of Israel.' And they would ask me, 'What is His name?' Then, what shall I say to them? They would continue ask, 'Who told you that you would be our leader? What is the name of the One who sent you?' Then, what shall I tell them? "

I can understand Moses' concern. Moses was in the Median desert for 40 years and worked just as an ordinary country shepherd. He was not a man of authority and power, but merely a forgotten laborer. Nobody elected him to their new leader and no earthly authority had approved him as the leader of the Israelites for the heavy mission ahead. However, God said to Moses, "I am who Am", which means "I will be what I Am". God said to Moses, "This is what you are to say to the Israelites, 'I Am (Jehovah)' has sent me to you."

What does "I am who Am" mean? It means that God is not dependent on anyone. God is SELF-Existence and Transcendent. God is absolute being, incomparable with us, who are relative beings. So, God has authority above heaven and earth as His name is "Jehovah".

Under the name of Jehovah there are eight sub-names of Jehovah -God.

1. Jehovah-Jireh: Provider
2. Jehovah-Rophe: Healer
3. Jehovah-Nisei: Banner of Victory
4. Jehovah-M'Kaddesh: Holy
5. Jehovah-Shalom: Peace
6. Jehovah-Rohi: Shepherd
7. Jehovah-Tsidkeme: Righteous
8. Jehovah-Shammah: God who is present in where we are and whose presence is in every place

I want to explain just one among those 8 names because of the limitation of time. Let me describe the meaning of Jehovah-Jireh, which means God is the provider. God who exists by Himself is our provider. There are times when we cannot find the way out from imminent danger or maneuver through other problems. We can find no alternatives, nor any solutions. During those difficult times, if we look to God, He will provide the way out, and He will be our provider. When Abraham was told to offer his only son as a burnt offering, Abraham obeyed and was about to give his son, Isaac, as a burnt offering. At that moment, God provided the lamb for the sacrifice. God had trapped the lamb in a bush and showed to Abraham the lamb as a substitute of Isaac. From that time on, Abraham referred to God as God, the provider: Jehovah -Jireh.

Jesus taught us to pray first, "Our Father who are in Heaven, Hallowed be Thy Name" to Glorify God's name. He is a Hallowed God; Elohim, the Almighty God; El-Shaddai, who is our perfect satisfaction; Jehovah, who alone can be called the living God; Jehovah-Jirah, who is our provider in times of adversity and the time of crisis. In Christ, we are adopted as Children of God and we call God as our Father. We have son/daughter-ship of God. It is like a slave being adopted as a son/daughter into a noble family. Since we are adopted as God's children we have i) A New Identity ii) A New Name iii) The Privilege to be heirs of God's glorious kingdom.

So, let us pray that the name of God would be lifted up highly. Let us also enjoy the full privilege of calling God as our Mighty provider, loving and compassionate Father.

We will have real joy and happiness
Psalm 51:1-12

Paul said, "The Kingdom of God is not a matter of eating and drinking, but of righteousness and peace and joy in the Holy Spirit." (Romans 14:7) We value highly the righteousness. Yes, the righteousness is very important issue in our lives. The theme of the Protestant Movement was the issue of righteousness as Martin Luther raised the flag, "The righteous shall live by faith". However, we can not ignore the importance of joy and peace in our lives. As Paul said in Romans 14:7, peace and Joy has same value as the righteousness in our Christian character because the Kingdom of God is not only the place that the righteous people go, but the place that we have a joy and the peace. The joy and peace should be present in our daily lives as we possess the kingdom of God among us and in our hearts.

Here is the word of Paul that he emphasizes the importance of joy in our lives in any circumstances: "Rejoice in the Lord always: and again I say, rejoice". Paul asked us to rejoice when he was in the deep dungeon at Rome as a prisoner. It means a lot to those who are facing adversities and difficulties when they couldn't be joyful with their normal mental capability.

With this message, Bible was not encouraging to ignore the grief process in the time of sorrow. The Israelites grieved 40 days when their leader Moses passed away. Even Jesus wept when His friend Lazarus died. However, as the wise man said, "There is a time for sorrow; there is a time for laugh". Grief and joy should be balanced timely. We couldn't do the balancing these two like a mathematical equation, but we make balance these two in some way. Basically, we should be joyful always in the Lord.

In today's message, I want to talk i) what does joy benefit to us? ii) how could we be joyful in any circumstances?

I. What Joy Benefit to our life?

First of all, I want to say that joy would help us to get along in a happy mood and it drives out discord. When there are a disagreement and conflicts between the husband and wife, employers and employees, in any relationship, even if they continue to disagree on some issues, they would still find the good resolution and balances options when there still are joy in their marriage, family, and the company. The proverb said, "A cheerful heart is the medicine of the body, but grief dries out our bones". It is not a metaphysical expression. It is true that the grief, conflicts, and bitter argument hurt the health and dries out bones. In on opposite, laughter brings Endorphin in our body and it release the stress from our brain to the nerves. Joy works as an excellent medicine and gives power for the body. So, when we are joyful, our soul will experience the jubilee and it makes our body healthy. Chares Spurgeon, a famous English preacher of the 19th Century, said, "joy is like a bird; let it fly in the open heavens, and let its music be heard by all men, joy is stimulation and so it urges us to be brave and face trials positively."

Secondly, joy affects others to stay happy and it attracts people. When we Christians are joyful together, non-believers would be attracted to us because they also want to be happy and joyful. There is proverb like this, "More flies are caught with a spoonful of honey than with a barrel of vinegar." With our joy, we influence others and draw them to the light. In the 2nd Corinthians 2:14-15, Paul used the word, "The fragrance of life". As an opposite concept, he used the word, "The smell of death". We Christians should be fragrance of life like a smell of roses that draws bird and bees to their nutrition.

II. What takes away our joy? / How could we restore our joy?

1. The trials can take away our joy/ Long perspective of life will restore joy

As the Hebrews said, when God gives us trial and discipline, we would be sorrowful because it is not pleasant. Trials can come in many ways-health problems, financial difficulties, break up marriages and persecution, etc. There are two reasons that God gives us trials; God's disciplinary chastising, and our own faulty sinful life. Either way, if we strongly believe that God would help us and take discipline in a positive way, we could maintain our serenity and continue to have a joy.

The first and most important secret of maintaining joy in the midst of discipline is to remember that the Lord disciplines those He loves and the result of discipline would be a fruit of righteousness and peace. (Hebrews 12:11)

Secondly, put things in perspective in a positive way.

Look at problems with God's long-term perspective. Romans 8:28 says, "In all things God works for the good of those who love him" So, think about the result in a positive way. God is excellent in making best out of it from everything. The specific event you thought as a sorrowful and painful will turn to the event that would help you and saves you in other times. No matter how big trials you have, God's intend for the discipline is to give us strength, not to destroy us. God's intend of giving trial is to form a positive character, which are patience, wisdom, and humbleness. It is like building a muscle as it says, "No pain, No gain".

Thirdly, trust God who would save you. Lord promised that, "If we call upon His name in the day of trouble, He would deliver us and honor us." (Psalm50:15) We can restore our joy when we trust God. When Job got the discipline of God harshly, he trusted the Lord who would make him as a better person and he believed that he would become like gold after the trial.

2. Sin can take away your joy/ Repentance and acceptance of God's unfailing forgiveness

Why people desire to involve in a sinful way of life? They thought that sin may stimulate them to have joyful life, which we call as 'pleasure'. Drug, sexual misbehavior, robbery, cheating, with all of these, they thought they would have a joy. By the contrast, those sins take away joy from our lives. Romans 2:9-10 reads, "Tribulation and anguish, upon every soul of men that does evil, of the Jew first, and also of the Gentile; but, glory, honor, and peace, to every man that worked good." Sin brings consequences. Not only that, it gives trouble to our souls. As a good example, we can tell the story of King David. When King David had affair with Bathsheba and had killed her husband, he had so much anguish in his soul and he loosed joy completely. Psalm 32:3-4 says, "When I kept silent, my bones wasted away through my groaning all day long. For day and night your hand was heavy upon me; my strength was sapped as in the heat of summer." How he restored his joy? When he truly repented and asked forgiveness, God forgave him and then he restored his joy. In Psalm 51: 12, King David asked, "Restore to the joy of salvation". Let me read few verses of Psalm 51, "Purge me with hyssop, and I shall be clean: wash me, and I shall be whiter than snow. Make me to hear joy and gladness; that the bones which thou hast broken may rejoice. Hide thy face from my sins, and blot out all mine iniquities. Crete in me a clean heart, O God; and renew a right spirit within me. Cast me not away from thy presence; and take not thy holy spirit from me. Restore unto me the joy of salvation; and uphold me with thy free spirit." King David finally could rejoice when he deeply repented his sin and accepted the forgiveness of God. God's forgiveness is always the resource of joy. Here, David asked not to take away the Spirit of God from him. It is true to have Spirit of God in our heart to restore the joy. Romans chapter 8 intensely contrasts the sinful human nature and the indwelling Spirit of God. It said, "And the Spirit of God in us produces an abundance of fruits: patience, kindness, goodness, love, peace and the abundance of life." If we live according to our sinful desires, we will be slaves of sins. But if we render ourselves to Christ and put ourselves totally in His welcoming Hands, the Spirit of God rules us. It allows us to have absolute freedom from sinful human desire. Once you accept Christ, you are dwelling in the Spirit of God and the Spirit of God dwells always in you. It is like Mercury in the thermometer. When it is hot the Mercury goes up, when it is cold the level of Mercury goes down. Spirit of God is working in you, when you accept Christ and this Spirit would guide, indwell, and control you heart. Whether you are lukewarm or cold toward Christ, just like the Mercury in the thermometer, the indwelling of the Spirit plummets. The gauge of the Spirit may go up and down according to your spiritual condition. However, the residing Spirit in you doesn't go anywhere. As we willingly love to live according to God's will, the Spirit of God restores our soul. Therefore, let us pray that Spirit of God renew us and restore our joy. The joy and happiness are the privileges that we can enjoy as we have new life in God, Jesus, and the Holy Spirit.

We will live bold and courageous life
Acts 1:1-11

I would like to talk what happened in the life of Christ's disciples after the ascension of Jesus Christ, especially after they had witnessed Christ' resurrection.

First, the disciples became courageous and devoted after they had seen their Lord's resurrection. Christ's disciples had several experiences that dramatically changed their lives in Jerusalem in just one week. One day there was triumph, the next day there was tragedy and the next day, a miracle. On one of those days, a large crowd came to welcome their Master. The disciples felt like they were in the king's cabinet. They should have been excited since they thought that their dream of the Messianic Jewish kingdom had been achieved. But, the very next day they witnessed their Master's extreme pain on the cross and execution. They were so frustrated and even terrified. On the way to return to their hometown, one of the followers of Christ expressed their frustration like this, "About Jesus of Nazareth, He was a prophet, powerful in word and deed before God and the people. We had hoped that He was going to redeem Israel. But, the chief priests and our rulers handed Him over to be sentenced to death and they crucified Him. And what is more, it was just three days ago that all of this took place. Then, some of our women amazed us when they went to the tomb early in the morning. They told us that they could not find the Master's body. They told us that they had even seen a vision of angels, who told the women that He was alive." (Luke 24: 19-24) These disciples just could not believe that Christ could be resurrected. They pondered what to do and were really frustrated. Consequently their dispositions were downcast. They felt that they were failures. Have you experienced this kind of frustration? You say to yourself, 'I put all of my energy into this project and I expected something to come out of the effort, but no pay off!' With a sigh of frustration, you might say, 'For what? For whom?'.

Fortunately, the story of the future of the disciples did not end there. Luke, the author of the Gospel of Luke was writing the second book as the series of the redemptive story, and his focus here was, "Then, What happened to the followers of Christ?"

Luke in his preface of the second series, which is Acts, stated, " In my former book, Theophilus, I wrote about all that Jesus began to do and to teach until the day He was taken up to heaven, after giving instructions through the Holy Spirit to the apostles he had chosen. After His suffering, He showed himself to these men and gave many convincing proofs that He was alive. He appeared to them over a period of forty days and spoke about the kingdom of God."(1-3)

If the suffering of Christ were the end of the story, there would be no Christianity in our history. As Christians we would not even be here today. The whole human history would have gone in another direction. The resurrection of Christ is the whole foundation of our belief. Although Christ had loved and did great miracles for people, Jesus had relatively little influence in His life, and He was able to hold onto only a few followers, only a few insignificant persons. Even those insignificant disciples had a shaky faith. As you had seen, when Christ their Master faced severe pain and death, not even one of the followers dared to stand up for their Master. After the crucifixion they all tried to go back to their hometown in a complete frustration and sorrow. However, after they became convinced that their Lord was raised, they became very influential and courageous in spreading the Gospel of Christ. Those who were shaky and coward before became courageous. When they started the church and spread the Gospel, they were only a few Galileans. However, their faith and preaching fortitude significantly influenced the world. In Bible tradition, it was said, "Thomas, the suspicious and doubting disciple went to India, to a far away country and gave his life to spread the Gospel. Peter was crucified upside down to preach the Gospel in Rome."

The first and the most important proof of Christ's resurrection is the life of His believers. Their courage and devotion proved that the resurrection of Christ was a real history. As Christ said in his parable of the mustard seed, the Christianity that was like a small insignificant seed grew up and became a huge tree whose branches hosted many nests for souls. What was the other significant things happened after they had witnessed the resurrection of Jesus Christ?

Secondly, the Holy Spirit that was poured on them on the day of Pentecost gave them the capability to communicate the word of God excellently. On one occasion, when Christ enjoyed the reunion with His disciples at the dinner table, Christ gave them this command, "Do not leave Jerusalem, but wait for the gift my Father promised, which you have heard me speak about. For John the Baptist baptized with water, but in a few days you will be baptized with the Holy Spirit." What happened then after that first Easter? Christ's first believers became filled with the Holy Spirit. They became very fluent in the using different languages when they preached the Gospel of Christ. They became international and were able to communicate the Gospel to everyone.

The focus here was not speaking unknown tongues but the Spirit's enabling them to communicate with all kinds of people world widely. Originally, humans spoke one language, perhaps Aramaic, I do not know. Different languages began to develop when humans started against God and attempted to make their name glorified. God disliked their attempt to build a high tower to reach heaven. So, God confused their language to scatter them. (Genesis 10:1-11) Therefore, the fact that the people could understand and heard the word of Disciples of Christ with their native tongues when the Spirit poured down unto them signified that the primary work of the Holy Spirit was to enable Christ's apostles to communicate to the world and to understand each other. God widened the Jewish Christ's disciples' narrow-mind. And now they were able to love all kinds of people.

After the resurrection, Christ immediately taught about the spiritual and universal kingdom of God. The disciples had a narrow-minded only concerned their country and asked Christ, "Lord, will you at this time restore the kingdom of Israel?" Christ answered to them, "It is not for you to know the times or dates the Father has set by his own authority. But you will receive power when the Holy Spirit comes on you; and you will be my witnesses in Jerusalem, and in all Judea and Samaria, and to the ends of the earth." Christ was not just referring to the geographical extension of Christianity neither disagreeing their love for their country. The main focus of Christ's recommendation was to confront the confines of Jewish nationalism and to make the disciples understand the universal love of God.

What happened, then, after their Lord was taken up to heaven? The apostles had changed their view of life and were enabled to love all kinds of people of the world, even different people. They preached the gospel to the world. After having started out as a seed of mustard, the apostles became influential throughout the whole world, spreading the gospel of love, spreading the gospel of peace and spreading the gospel of salvation to the world. The witnesses of the Christ's resurrection became new and they became bold, broad-minded. In old days, you may be a coward and narrow-minded, but now the new has come and you are new creatures of God who could live bold and broad-minded. Apostle Paul told his spiritual son, "For God did not give us a spirit of timidity, but the spirit of power, of love and of self-discipline." (2nd Timothy 1:7)

We will inherit God's Kingdom
John chapter 3, Revelation chapter 21, 22

The Kingdom of God! There are such a broad topics in this concept!

What is the kingdom of God? When is it coming? Where is it? How can I get there? Is it futuristic or for now? Will it be completed now or in the Pre-Millennium or in Mid-Millennium or in the Post Millennium? Is the earth going to be preserved when the kingdom of God comes? Where is the Kingdom going to be established, in Heaven, where? There are many questions to be answered. It is very important to have the correct Biblical concept about all those topics pertaining to the heavenly kingdom.

Do you remember the tragedy that happened in San Diego, California where the sect of the "Heaven's Gate" committed mass suicide? I personally could not understand how it could happen because all of those people involved in the events were from the intellectual and educated people. How those people could be misled by such childish thoughts and gave up their lives, I mean killing themselves! I am not sitting in judgment seat nor trying to tell you how foolish were they. Instead, I want to tell you how important it is to have a balanced and sound Biblical view regard to all concepts that pertain to the "Heavenly Kingdom"

Using the picture of the Garden of Eden, the Apostle John described the kingdom of God in his book of Revelations. (Chapter 21 and 22) When John was in his old age, he was an outcast from society and was sent to the lonely and distant island named, Batmo. He received a revelation from God in that lonely Island and wrote the Book of Revelations. Two chapters of Revelations 21and 22 has the textbook passages on the subject of 'The Kingdom of God". With those two scriptures and Genesis chapter 1 and 2, we can safely arrive at the concept of the heavenly kingdom. If our concept of the heavenly kingdom is based upon these books, we will not become lost and be misled by different sects.

What is your picture of the 'Kingdom of God'? When I gave the Sunday-school lesson for the children of meddlers, I asked them to draw their picture of the heavenly kingdom. I just told them that the kingdom of God is "THE HAPPIEST PLACE." Some drew pictures like DISNEYLAND. Some drew Mommy and Daddy playing with him or her at the playground. Their creativity made me surprise.

What is your picture of the heavenly kingdom? I have four important concepts to present this morning regarding the kingdom of God.

First, the kingdom of Heaven will be like Garden of Eden.

Nobody who is living now has experienced the "Heavenly kingdom" and so it is hard to tell what it is. However, God gives us a pictorial view of the heavenly kingdom through the Bible to help us arrive at the idea and the basic understanding about His kingdom.

The Garden of Eden in the Book of Genesis gives us a fine picture of the heavenly kingdom. Eden means "the happiness" As the name of the place implies, the Garden of Eden is the happiest garden. We refer to this garden as Paradise. Paradise is not the heavenly kingdom, but it gives us the picture of heavenly kingdom. As parents want to provide the happiest life for their children, our Father in heaven wants to provide us the happiest garden. So, He created the Garden of Eden.

What was in this exceptional garden, which is the picture of the kingdom of God that we would enjoy living in?

- God make us able to have eternal life by giving us the 'Tree of Life', which was in the center of the Garden.
- God gave us plenty of food and trees that produce all kinds of good fruit
- God gave us beautiful environment
- God gave all kinds of gems and pearls and it was free to claim

- God gave us four rivers, which are the expression to be prosperous
- God created a happy family and it was the group, and fellowship the He instituted.
- God gave us pleasant and plenty job to do

With this picture of the Garden of Eden, the Apostle John described the kingdom of God in his book of Revelation. (Chapter 21 and 22) How does the Apostle describe the kingdom of God in his revelation? Revelation 22:1-5 said, "Then the angel showed me the river of the water of life, as clear as crystal, flowing from the throne of God and of the Lamb down in the middle of the great street of the city. On each side of the river stood the tree of life, bearing twelve crops of fruit, yielding its fruit every month. And the leaves of the tree are for the healing of the nations. No longer, there will be any curse....There will be no more night. They will not need the light of lamp or light of the sun, for the Lord God will give them light." In new heaven, there will be no more death, or mourning or crying because the old order of things has passed away. Heaven will be a new place, because the first earth had passed away. Revelation 21: 1, 4 says, "Then I saw a new heaven and a new earth, for the first heaven and the first earth had passed away, and there was no longer any sea. I saw a Holy city, the New Jerusalem, coming down out of heaven from God, prepared as a bride beautifully dressed for her husband. He will wipe out every tear from their eyes. There will be no more death or mourning or crying or pain for the old order of things has passed away."

The new heaven is the new realm that the children of God were waiting for and every human being, all creatures, even trees eagerly desire as it was expressed in Romans 8: 21-24a, "The creation itself will be liberated from its bondage to decay and brought into the glorious freedom of the children of God. We know that the whole creation has been groaning as in the pains of childbirth right up to the present time. Not only they, but also we ourselves, the recipients of the first fruits of the Spirit, groan inwardly as we wait eagerly for our adoption as children of God and the redemption of our bodies. For in this hope we were saved."

Second, the Kingdom of God is everlasting.

Throughout the Old Testament, God had given us a clear picture about what the kingdom would be like. Daniel 2:44 says: "The God of heaven will set up a kingdom that will never be destroyed, it will be established forever." Kingdoms in this earth rise and fall. However, the kingdom of God will be established forever and His reign will be just and righteous.

Third, the Character of the king in God's kingdom is righteous and peace lover.

In the New Holy city, God is the King and we are the people under His reign. (Chapter 21 verses 1-3) To have a happy life, we need a good ruler. In the Book of Revelation, along with other old prophesies, the new king is described as righteous and prince of peace.

The prophet, Isaiah, gave us the portrait of the king in heave at Isaiah 8: 6-7, "For to us a child is born, to us a son is given, and the government will be on his shoulders. And he will be called 'Wonderful counselor, Mighty God, Everlasting Father, Prince of peace, there will be no end. He will reign on David's throne and over his kingdom, establishing and upholding the kingdom with justice and righteousness from that time on and forever."

What is the character of the new ruler, the king in heaven in this verse? Wonderful counselor, prince of peace, just and righteous! Isaiah 11: 1-9 also supports the character of the king in heaven as righteous. It says, "Righteousness will be his belt and faithfulness the sash around his waist. The wolf will live with the lamb. The infant will play near the hole of the cobra, and the young child will put his hand into the viper's nest." The kingdom of God is a peaceful and harmonious land, where there is neither harm nor destruction because the 'Prince of Peace/

Righteous King' is reigning there. Fourthly, the Kingdom of God is both futuristic and for the present as well

Fourth, the Kingdom of God both futuristic and present. All of those pictures that were given and prophesied by the Old Testament are futuristic and will be fulfilled at the end of the ages with the second coming of Jesus Christ. Jesus promised that He would return at the end of the age to establish His kingdom, and it will be accompanied with dramatic, chaotic and radical physical phenomena as Jesus prophesied at Luke 21:25-28. It says, "There shall be signs in the sun, and in the moon and in the stars; and upon the earth distress of nations, with perplexity; the sea and the waves roaring." All those are supernatural cosmic wonders happening in this earth when the days come in the future.

However, the kingdom of God is not only futuristic, but it is also in the present. The first message of our Lord, Jesus Christ, was the nearness of His kingdom. He said, "The kingdom of God is near. Repent!" When He sent His disciples into towns to minister to the people, Jesus told them, "Proclaim that the kingdom of God has come near to you." The kingdom is not just someplace away from us. It is something near, into which every human can enter now. IT IS NOT JUST SOMETHING EXTERNALLY IMPOSED FROM OUTSIDE, IT IS ALSO THE REIGN OF GOD IN THE HUMAN HEART WHEREVER OBEDIENCE TO GOD IS FOUND. It is a realm that we can enter now, a realm that is possible now in the present, if the righteousness of God and the righteous values of Christ are applied.

There was one occasion when the disciples asked, 'Lord, where is the kingdom of God?'. Jesus answered, "The Kingdom of God is not here or there. The Kingdom of GOD IS IN THE MIDST OF YOU." That phrase means God's kingdom is in your hearts and amongst you right now. Traditionally, the kingdom of God had been understood as a future reign of Christ which would be established by His dramatic second coming, which is true and Biblical. However, we also have to understand the kingdom of God is for the present time as well. When we live according to God's grace and love for each other, we will realize that the Kingdom is here right now in our heart and among us. Therefore, instead of looking solely to the future for the occurrence of the heavenly kingdom, we should also search for the kingdom of God in our present life.

In the future after we die or when Christ comes, our earthly body does not inherit the heavenly kingdom. However, God will transform our body as a spiritual and glorious body. He will take our whole being, not only our spirit, to heaven. While we are in this world, right in the present time, the Spirit of God transforms us and makes us as new born creature to possess heaven in our hearts and in our relationships with others.

Let me give one example to illustrate how a loving heart and a loving disposition toward others transform a physical situation into a heavenly result. I would like to refer to the Dickens novel, "A Christmas Story". By serving others, Scrooge savored the heavenly kingdom right then and there in his heart. In his spiritual awakening from a dream, Scrooge realizes that when he dies, he would not be able to take any earthly possessions with him and his earthly body would perish. So, Scrooge gave those material possessions to serve and love others. As a result, he had a heavenly joy and experienced the happiness of possessing the Kingdom of God in his heart. The Spirit of God came into a person and transformed Scrooge, who only loved material things and hated his neighbors. The reverberations of that joy are reflected in the change in attitude of Scrooge from a grumpy codger to a happy philanthropist. That generous nature forecasts the kingdom of God. I believe that, on the last day when body and soul are reunited, Scrooge would enter into the Kingdom of God, continuing in his philanthropic ways.

The future Kingdom will be the extension of Scrooge's goodness in this earthly kingdom. We must always remember, therefore, that we not only have the promise of a futuristic kingdom of God, but we also have the kingdom of God in our heart and among our present relationship with others. We have the joy, the light, and the hope that Christ gave us right now in this present life and great hope for the future kingdom. Hallelujah. God promised that we Christian, who is born anew, will inherit the Kingdom of God. Since we have a new life, we will have privilege to enter the kingdom of God. We also have privilege to enjoy, experience the light and joy of the kingdom of God now.

내영혼이 은총입어 중한 죄짐 벗고 보니

Amazing Grace

Amazing Grace! How sweet the sound
That saved a wretch like me!
I once was lost, but now am found
Was blind, but now I see.

'Twas Grace that taught my heart to fear,
And Grace my fears relieved.
How precious did that Grace appear
The hour I first believed.

Through many dangers, toils, and snares
I have already come.
'Tis Grace hath brought me safe thus far
And Grace will lead me home.

The Lord has promised good to me.
His Word my hope secures.
He will my shield and portion be
As long as life endures.

When we've been there ten thousand years
Bright shining as the sun,
We've no less days to sing God's praise
Than when we'd first begun.

Songwriters: TRADITIONAL, JOSEPH SHABALALA, PAUL SIMON

© Public Domain[3]

---

[3] https://www.bing.com/search?q=amazing grace lyrics&pc=cosp&ptag=G6C19N1234D020119A98C4AF66BD (Accessed on 5/16/2020)

Lightning Source UK Ltd.
Milton Keynes UK
UKHW011013210820
368606UK00001B/80